Star of Light

Patricia St John

Revised by Mary Mills

Illustrated by Gary Rees

Scripture Union

©Patricia M. St. John 1953
First published 1953
This revised edition first published 2001, reprinted 2002

Scripture Union, 207–209 Queensway, Bletchley, Milton
Keynes MK2 2EB
Email: info@scriptureunion.org.uk
Website: www.scriptureunion.org.uk

ISBN 1 85999 510 1

Printed and bound in Great Britain by
Creative Print and Design (Wales) Ebbw Vale.

Scripture Union is an international Christian charity
working with churches in more than 130 countries,
providing resources to bring the good news about
Jesus Christ to children, young people and families and
to encourage them to develop spiritually through the
bible and prayer.

As well as our network of volunteers, staff and associates
who run holidays, church-based events and school
Christian groups, we produce a wide range of
publications and support those who use our resources
through training programmes.

Contents

Revised edition

It is over fifty years since the first edition of Patricia St John's *Star of Light* was published. It has been reprinted many times and has become a classic of its time.

In this new edition, Mary Mills has sensitively adapted the language of the book for a new generation of children, while preserving Patricia St John's skill as a storyteller.

Titles by Patricia M. St. John

THE TANGLEWOODS' SECRET

TREASURES OF THE SNOW

STAR OF LIGHT

RAINBOW GARDEN

THE SECRET OF THE FOURTH CANDLE

THE MYSTERY OF PHEASANT COTTAGE

For older readers:

NOTHING ELSE MATTERS

THE VICTOR

I NEEDED A NEIGHBOUR

For younger readers:

THE OTHER KITTEN

FRISKA, MY FRIEND

Chapter One

Kinza

A little girl came running down the side of the mountain one mid-day in spring. Pulling her cotton dress around her knees, she skipped as lightly as a lamb on her bare brown feet, leaping over the bright orange marigolds which shone up at her. Baby goats jumped among the wild flowers, and the storks had begun to build their nests on the tops of the thatched houses.

Rahma was seven years old. She was small because she didn't have enough to eat. Her step-father and his elder wife didn't like her and some-times beat her. Her clothes were very ragged, and she had to work very hard. But today she was going to have a treat, and nothing could spoil her happiness. She had been asked to look after the goats alone while her brother went on some mysterious trip with their mother.

She was free and alone with just the goats and storks for company – two whole hours to play in the sunshine with the goat kids, with no one to shout at her, or make her grind the millstone, or carry heavy buckets of water.

She spotted Hamid, her brother, rounding up a couple of mischievous black kids who were trying to get into a patch of young wheat. Spring was making them feel excited and they were jumping about all over the place. Hamid joined in with them and then Rahma, too, her smooth dark hair blowing about her face, her black eyes shining brightly.

Laughing and shouting together, they steered the kids away from the patch of wheat and on to the open hillside where the rest of the flock was scattered. Then Hamid turned, surprised, to look at his little sister. He had not often seen her so happy and carefree, for country girls were taught to behave themselves properly.

"What have you come for?" he asked.

"To look after the goats. Mother wants you."

"Why?"

"I don't know – she wants you to go somewhere. She has been crying and looking at little sister. I think perhaps little sister is ill."

Her sparkling eyes looked sad as she remembered her mother's tears, for she loved her mother – only the sunshine and freedom had made her forget all about them.

"All right," said Hamid, "but take good care of the goats. Here's a stick for you."

He turned away and climbed the valley between

the two green arms of the mountains. He walked fast because he did not want to keep his mother waiting, but he did not skip or look about him as Rahma had done, for his mind was full of questions.

Why did his mother look so worried and full of fear these days? Why was she always hiding away his baby sister, keeping her out of sight whenever she heard her husband or the older wife approaching? Of course, neither of them had ever really liked baby sister, but they knew she was there, so why hide her? Mother even seemed afraid of him and Rahma playing with the baby nowadays. She would drive them away, and hide in a corner of the room, her little daughter clasped against her, and always that fear in her eyes. Was it evil spirits she feared? Or poison? Hamid did not know, but perhaps today his mother would tell him. He walked faster.

He sighed as he climbed the hill, because until a few months ago his mother had never looked frightened, and he and Rahma had never been knocked about or considered in the way. They had lived with their mother and their own father, who loved them, in a little thatched home down the valley. There had been three other curly-headed children younger than Rahma, but they had started coughing and grown thin. When the snow fell, and there was hardly any bread or fuel, they grew weaker and died within a few weeks of each other. Their little bodies were buried on the eastern slope of the mountain facing the sunshine, and marigolds and daisies grew on their graves.

Their father coughed that winter, too, but no one

took any notice because, after all, a man must earn his living. So he went on working, and ploughed his fields in spring, and sowed his grain. Then he came home one night and said he could work no more. Until the following autumn he lay on the rush mat and grew weaker. Zohra, his wife, and Hamid and Rahma gathered in the ripened corn, and gleaned what they could so they could buy him food, but it was no use. He died, leaving his wife, still young and beautiful, a poor widow with two little children.

They sold the house and the goats and the hens and the patch of corn, and went to live with their grandmother. A few months later little sister was born, bringing fresh hope and sunshine to the family. They called her Kinza, which means "treasure", and everyone loved and cuddled her. Yet, strangely, she never played or clapped her hands like other babies. She slept a lot, and often seemed to lie staring at nothing. Hamid sometimes wondered why she didn't seem pleased with the bunches of bright flowers he picked for her.

When Kinza was a few months old, a man offered to marry their mother. She accepted at once, because she had no work and no more money to buy food for her three children, and the family moved to their new home.

It was not a very happy home. Si Mohamed, the husband, was already married to an older wife, but she had never had any children, so he wanted another wife. He did not mind taking Hamid too, because a boy of nine would be useful to look after the goats. He also thought Rahma could be a useful little slave girl about the house; but he could not see that a baby was any use at all, and he wanted to give Kinza away.

"Many childless women will be glad of a girl," he said, "and why should I bring up another man's baby?"

But young Zohra had burst into tears and refused to do any work until he changed his mind, so he rather crossly agreed to let Kinza stay for a while. No more was said about it – unless perhaps something had been said during the past few weeks – something that Hamid and Rahma had not heard. Could that be why their mother held Kinza so close, and looked so frightened?

A voice above him called to him to run, and he looked up. His mother was standing under an old twisted olive tree that threw its shade over a well. She carried two empty buckets, and baby Kinza was tied on her back with a cloth. She seemed in a great hurry about something.

"Come quick, Hamid," she said impatiently. "How slowly you come up the path! Hide the buckets in the bushes – I only brought them as an excuse to leave the house, in case Fatima should want to know where I was going. Now, come with me."

"Where to, Mother?" asked the little boy, very surprised.

"Wait till we get round the corner of the mountain," replied his mother, leading the way up the steep, green grass, and walking very fast. "People will see us from the well and will tell Fatima where we have gone. Follow quickly. I'll tell you soon."

They hurried on until they were hidden from the

village and overlooking another valley. Zohra sat down and laid her baby in her lap.

"Look well at her, Hamid," she said. "Play with her and show her the flowers."

Hamid stared long and hard into the strangely old, patient face of his little sister, but she did not stare back or return his smile. She seemed to be looking at something very far away, and did not see him at all. Suddenly feeling very afraid, he flicked his hand in front of her eyes, but she didn't move or blink.

"She's blind," he whispered at last. His lips felt dry and his face was white.

His mother nodded, and quickly stood up. "Yes," she replied, "she's blind. I've known it for some time, but I haven't told Fatima and my husband because they will probably take her away from me. Why should they be bothered with another man's blind child? She can never work, and she will never marry..."

She started to cry, and tears blinded her as she stumbled on the rough path. Hamid caught hold of her arm.

"Where are we going, Mother?" he asked her again.

"To the saint's tomb," answered his mother, hurrying on, "up behind the next hill. They say he is a very powerful saint and has healed many people, but Fatima has never given me the chance to go. Now she thinks I'm drawing water, and we must return with the buckets full. I wanted you to come with me, because it's a lonely path and I was afraid to go by myself."

They climbed silently to a small cave that had

been hollowed out of the rock. There was a bush outside with many dirty, screwed-up pieces of paper tied to its branches. These all told tales of sorrow and sickness. People brought their burdens to the bones of this dead man, and they all went home unhealed and uncomforted.

They laid Kinza at the mouth of the cave, then Zohra lifted herself up again, calling on the name of a god whom she didn't know, and the prophet Mohammed. It was her last hope. As she prayed a cloud passed over the sun and a cold shadow fell on the baby. She shivered and began to cry and reached out for her mother's arms. Zohra gazed eagerly into her little daughter's face for a moment, and then picked her up with a disappointed sigh. God had not listened, for Kinza was still blind.

Hamid and his mother almost ran down the hill. They were late, and the sun was already setting behind the mountains. The storks flew past with their rattling cry, black against the sky. Hamid was angry and bitterly disappointed. What was the good of it? Kinza would never see. God did not seem to care, and the dead saint would do nothing to help. Perhaps he wasn't interested in baby girls.

They reached the well in silence. Hamid drew the water for his mother, gave her the buckets, then dashed off down the valley to collect Rahma and the goats. He met them half-way up the hill, for Rahma was afraid of the evening shadows and had wanted to get home. She held her brother's hand, and the goats, who also wanted to go home, huddled against their legs.

"Where did you go?" asked Rahma.

"To the saint's tomb," answered Hamid.

"Rahma, our little sister is blind. Her eyes see nothing but darkness – that's why Mother hides her away. She does not want Fatima and Si Mohamed to know."

Rahma stood still, horrified. "Blind?" she echoed, "and the saint – couldn't he make her see?"

Hamid shook his head. "I don't think that saint is much good," he said rather boldly. "Mother went there before, when Father coughed, but nothing happened. Father died."

"It is the will of God," said Rahma, and shrugged her shoulders. Then, clinging close together because night was falling, they climbed the hill, and the goats' eyes gleamed like green lanterns in the dark.

"I hate the dark," whispered Rahma with a little shiver.

But Hamid stared up into the deep blue sky.

"I love the stars," he said.

Chapter Two

The secret revealed

They reached the village ten minutes later and passed by the dark huts. Through open doors glowing charcoal gleamed cheerfully in clay pots, and families squatted round their evening meal by dim lamp-light. But as they came near their own house they could hear the angry voice of Fatima, the older wife, shouting at their mother.

Fatima hated the new wife and her three children and made life as hard as she could for them in every possible way. She was bent and wrinkled by long years of hard work, and Zohra was still young and beautiful. Fatima had longed in vain for a baby, while Zohra had had six. So perhaps it wasn't surprising that the older woman was so jealous, and had been so angry at their coming to live in the house. She showed her hatred by sitting cross-legged on the mattress like a queen all day and making Zohra and Rahma work like slaves. Zohra had only escaped to the well because Fatima had fallen asleep – but unfortunately she had not slept for long. Furious at finding the young woman not there, she had sent a neighbour's child to spy out for her. So Zohra, carrying her buckets, had arrived home to find that Fatima knew all about her expedition.

"Wicked, deceitful, lazy one!" shouted Fatima. "You can't deceive me. Give me that child! Let me see for myself why you hide her away, and hold her so secretly, and creep with her to the tomb. Give me her, I say! I insist on having her."

She snatched the baby roughly from Fatima's grasp and carried her to the light, and the mother sighed and let her empty arms fall to her sides. After all, Fatima must know soon. They could not hide it much longer, and she had better find out for herself.

The frightened children squatted in the shadows by the wall, their dark eyes very big. The hut was silent as Fatima passed her hands over the baby's limbs, and stared into Kinza's still face. Hamid, holding his breath, heard little sounds he had never noticed before – the slow, rhythmical munching of the ox in the stall, the rustle of straw as the kids nuzzled against their mothers, and the soft crooning of roosted hens.

Then the silence was broken by a triumphant cackle of laughter from the old woman, and Kinza, whose ears were very sensitive to loud noises and angry voices, gave a frightened cry. Fatima picked her up and almost flung her back into her mother's lap.

16

"Blind," she announced, "blind as night! And you knew – you knew all the time! You brought her here to your husband's house to be a burden on us all for ever – never to work, never to marry. You hid her away in case we found out. Oh, most deceitful of women! Our husband shall know about this tonight. Now – get up and prepare his supper, and you, Rahma, blow up the charcoal. When he has eaten his food we shall hear what he has to say."

The frightened little girl jumped up and set to work with the bellows till the flames leaped from the glowing coals and flung strange shadows on the walls. Zohra, trembling, laid her baby in the swinging wooden cradle that hung from a beam, and set to work to mash the beans and beat in the oil, for her husband had gone to speak to a neighbour, and would be home any time now. They were only just ready when they heard his firm steps coming along the path, and a moment later he appeared in the doorway – a tall man with black eyes and a black beard and a hard, cruel mouth. He wore a long garment made from dark home-spun goat's wool, with a white turban wound around his head. He did not speak to his wives or his step-children but sat cross-legged in front of the low, round table and signalled for the food to be set before him. If he noticed Fatima's triumph, and the white, scared faces of Zohra and the children, he said nothing.

Zohra set the hot dish in the centre of the table and the silent family gathered round. There were no spoons, but she broke two large pieces of bread for her husband and Fatima and three small pieces

17

for herself, Hamid and Rahma.

"In the name of God," they murmured as they scooped their bread in the centre dish, for they hoped the words would drive away evil spirits who might be lurking round the table. Sometimes at mid-day when the sun was shining Rahma forgot to say them, but she never forgot at night, for the flickering shadows and dark corners made her feel afraid. Evil spirits seemed very real and near after the lamps had been lit. And certainly tonight the little home was full of evil spirits – dark spirits of jealousy and anger and hatred and cruelty and fear. Even little Kinza in her hanging cradle seemed to feel the atmosphere, and wailed fretfully.

Si Mohamed frowned.

"Stop that noise," he growled. "Pick her up."

The mother obeyed and sat down again with her baby held very closely against her. Fatima waited a moment until her husband had finished eating, then she held out her arms.

"Give that child to me," she said threateningly, and Zohra handed over her baby and burst into tears.

"What is the matter?" said Si Mohamed irritably. His wives might quarrel all they pleased – wives always did quarrel – but he disliked them doing it in front of him. He had been ploughing all day and was tired.

"Yes, what is the matter indeed!" sneered Fatima, and she held out the baby at arm's length so that the lamp-light suddenly shone straight on to her face. But Kinza neither screwed up her eyes nor turned away from it. Si Mohamed stared at her directly.

18

"Blind!" cried Fatima, as she had shouted before. "Blind, blind, blind! And Zohra knew it – she has deceived us all."

"I didn't," sobbed Zohra, rocking to and fro.

"You did," shouted the old woman.

"Silence, you women," said their husband sternly, and the quarrel stopped immediately. Once again, there was silence in the dim hut. Rahma suddenly felt cold with fear, and crept closer to the dying charcoal. Her step-father looked very closely at Kinza's tiny face, flashed the light in front of it and jerked his hand towards it, until he was satisfied that the old woman spoke the truth.

"Truly," he agreed, "she is blind."

But the dreaded outburst of rage never came. He handed Kinza back to her mother, half-closed his eyes, and lit a long, thin pipe. He sat puffing away in silence for some time, until the hut was filled with sickly fumes, and then he said,

"Blind children can be very profitable. Keep that baby carefully. She may bring us much money."

"How?" asked Zohra nervously, her arms tightening around her baby.

"By begging," replied her husband. "Of course, we cannot take her begging ourselves, for I am an honourable man. But there are beggars who would be glad to hire her to sit with them in the markets. People feel sorry for blind children, and give generously. I believe I know of one who would pay to borrow her when she is a little older."

Zohra said nothing – she dared not. But Hamid and Zohra gave each other long rebellious looks across the table. They knew the beggar of whom their step-father spoke – an old man dressed in filthy old rags, who swore horrible oaths. They did not want their precious Kinza to go to that old man. He would certainly ill-treat her and frighten her.

Their step-father saw the look through half-closed eyelids. He clapped his hands sharply.

"To bed, you children," he ordered, "quick!"

They got up hurriedly, mumbled goodnight, and scuttled into dark corners of the room.

There were low mattresses laid along the wall. Curling themselves up on these, they pulled strips of blanket over them and fell fast asleep.

Hamid never knew why he woke that night, for he usually slept soundly till sunrise; but at about two in the morning he suddenly sat up in bed, wide awake. A patch of bright moonlight was shining through the window on to Kinza's cradle, and she was moaning and stirring in her sleep.

Hamid slipped from his mattress and stood beside her. Suddenly a great wave of protective tenderness seemed to come sweeping over him. She was so small, so patient and so defenceless. Well, he would see to it that no harm came to her. All his life he would guide her through her darkness, and protect her with his love. His heart swelled for a moment, and then he remembered that he was only a boy himself and completely under his step-father's control. They might take Kinza away from him, and then his love would be powerless to reach her.

Was there no stronger love to shelter her, no more certain light to lead her? He did not know.

Chapter Three

Si Mohamed makes a deal

Blind Kinza sat in the doorway of her hut and lifted her small face to the sunshine. It was Thursday, and on Thursday Kinza went to work. She was two-and-a-half years old now, and quite old enough, in her step-father's opinion, to earn her living like the rest of them.

She sat still and patient, her weak legs folded under her, her hands clasped quietly in her lap. It was quite early, and Hamid, who carried her to her job, had taken the cow to pasture and he would not be back for a while. In the meantime she was free to enjoy herself, and Kinza enjoyed herself quite a lot in her own way.

As long as the sun shone and the weather was fine, she was, on the whole, a happy little child. As she had never seen the light she could not miss it, and there were many good things to feel. There was the warmth and shelter of her mother's lap, the clasp of her brother's strong arms, and the wet noses of the kids when they nuzzled her hands. There was the touch of sun on her body and the wind on her face. Sometimes she was allowed to sit by her mother as she sorted the corn, and one of Kinza's greatest treats was to pick up handfuls of worn husks and let them slip through her fingers.

There were lovely things to hear, too, and she knew now that Hamid was coming towards her, from the particular sound of his bare feet on the dry mud. She held up her arms and gave a delighted squeak. Hamid picked her up and tied her firmly on his back.

"Market day, little sister," he announced. "Have you had some breakfast?"

Kinza nodded. Half an hour ago she had drunk a bowlful of sweet black coffee and eaten a hunk of brown bread. It was the best breakfast she knew, and she had really enjoyed it.

"Come then," said Hamid, and they set off together, keeping under the olive trees to begin with, because by nine o'clock in the summer the sun was blazing hot. But very soon they left the trees behind them, and the path to market ran between wheat-fields ripe for harvest, where the air smelled of poppies. The sound of the wind rustling through the corn made her sleepy, and Kinza laid her head on her brother's shoulder, and shut her eyes.

There were many people on the path that morning, and as they reached the market-place the crowds became thicker. It was an area of burnt yellow grass, shaded by eucalyptus trees, and the sellers sat cross-legged on the ground, with their goods piled up in front of them while the buyers tramped around them. Kinza hated it. She hated the jostling and the jolting and the noise, the dust that made her sneeze, the flies that crawled over her face and the fleas that bit her legs. Most of all she hated the moment when Hamid left her in the care of the old beggar.

But Hamid, to make it easier for her, had worked out a plan. During the week, he tried to beg, borrow or steal a small coin and he would exchange it in the market on Thursday morning for a lump of sticky green candy, covered with nuts. And licking that candy was the biggest treat Kinza knew.

Hamid knew the market-place very well, and made his way to the patch of sand where Kinza and the beggar sat side by side. He made sure he got there before the beggar to give him time to settle Kinza and let her eat the green candy. Hamid took a few secret licks himself first, and then handed it over, warm and wet, to his sister. She clasped it in her right hand, loving its sweet stickiness, and began to lick it all over, going round and round it with the tip of her little pink tongue. In her left hand she held tightly to the hem of Hamid's tunic, in case the roaring crowd should pull him away from her.

They had not been there long before the old beggar came shuffling towards them, with a coloured drum in his hand. He was amazingly dirty and old, and his patched coat was falling to pieces. Hamid kissed his hand politely and received the coin that was paid to his step-father each week for the loan of Kinza. But instead of dismissing him crossly as he usually did, the old beggar spoke to him.

"When your father comes down to buy," he growled, "tell him I have business with him."

Hamid nodded, freed himself gently from Kinza's grasp, and ran off. Kinza, finding herself left alone, started to cry, until the old beggar noticed and slapped her for it.

Her work was not very difficult during the early part of the day. All she had to do was to sit with her small face lifted to the light so that everyone could see she was blind, and hold out her hand. The old beggar sat beside her, thumping his drum to make people look at her, and chanting and swaying. Many people felt sorry for the tiny white-faced child, and gave her coins which she handed to her master. So they sat until noon, and the sun rose higher, and the dust and the flies grew thicker. The crowds wandered around them and the stray dogs sniffed them. Sometimes people tripped right over her.

At noon Kinza's master gave her a piece of dark rye-bread and a cup of water, and because she had collected quite a lot of money during the morning he gave her a squashed plum. It was delicious. She sucked all her ten fingers in turn so that she didn't lose one drop of juice.

The afternoon was harder than the morning, for by two o'clock Kinza began to grow sleepy. Her dark head, tied up in its cotton cloth, began to nod heavily, and her eyes just would not keep open. She longed for her mother's lap, but all she could do was lean against the old man's rags to rest her weary head.

24

But only for a few minutes. He saw what had happened and angrily jerked her upright. Feeling dazed, she rubbed her knuckles in her eyes, stretched herself and tumbled forwards. Once again he jerked her back, slapped her and propped her up against him. So, with her outstretched hand supported by the other, she sat begging, half-asleep, until the beggar suddenly got up and she fell over sideways.

He sat her up with an impatient bump. "Bad child!" he growled. "Sit and beg till I come back."

He had got up because, on the outskirts of the crowd, he had seen the tall figure of Kinza's step-father looking about for him. The farmer would not wish to speak to the beggar in the open market, so they met behind a huge eucalyptus tree and stood talking.

"You wanted me?" asked the farmer.

"Yes," said the old beggar. "I'm leaving the village. The country people are growing greedy and are giving less to honourable beggars, so I'm going to the big town on the coast, with my wife. The great feast will soon be here, and they say beggars grow rich in the streets of the town. Now this is what I want to say. Give me that blind child of yours. You are not a beggar, and you can never make use of her, but she makes a lot of money for me. My wife will look after her, and I will pay you a good sum for her."

Kinza's step-father hesitated. He knew that he was plotting a very wicked thing, but he needed money badly. His cow had strayed into a neighbour's corn and had been put in the cows' prison. He had to pay a lot of money to get it back again.

His harvest was poor this year, and Kinza, while she earned a little, was and always would be an extra mouth to feed.

Si Mohamed refused to listen to his conscience. After all, Kinza was not his child. Hamid was eleven, almost a man, and could soon be left to earn his own living, and Rahma could be married off in three or four years. But this might be the first and last chance he would ever have of getting rid of Kinza.

"How much will you give me?" he said at last.

The beggar mentioned a small sum. The farmer said that was not nearly enough. The beggar shouted back and they bargained angrily for some time. Nobody took much notice, for that is the way prices are fixed in the country. They finally agreed on a price that was exactly half-way between what both had asked in the first place.

"Right," said the beggar at last. "I'll be leaving the village at dawn on the first day of the week. When you hand over the child I will hand over the money, and it shall be done in the presence of witnesses."

Though neither showed it, both were pleased. The old beggar fought his way back to Kinza, hoping she had managed to collect some coins while he had been away. But she had done nothing of the sort. She had crept into a patch of shade and lay fast asleep, curled up in a ball like a tired kitten.

Chapter Four

Zohra makes a plan

Hamid stood on the outskirts of the market, his thin brown face turned upward, his bright, dark eyes fixed on the top of the mosque, waiting for the priest to appear and shout the four o'clock prayer-call. This was the time Kinza was released and he could carry her off, safe for another week.

The crowd was thinning now, and Hamid could spot his sister sitting in a sad little heap beside her master. She was in disgrace because she had fallen asleep, and Hamid was impatient to rescue her.

The mosque was the village temple – a building with a square tower dazzling white against the blue sky. A golden crescent gleamed from the top. At last the old bearded priest appeared and sent his chanted call ringing out across the market-place.

"There is one God," he cried, "and Mohammed

is his prophet."

Faithful Moslems flocked to the temple or took off their shoes and prayed where they stood, facing east, bowing low and sometimes kneeling with their foreheads on the ground.

The moment Hamid caught sight of the priest, he raced across the market, kissed the old beggar's hand in greeting, and snatched up his little sister.

He had brought her a doughnut. She clutched it eagerly and took a mouthful. In the joy of feeling his arms safe about her once more, she forgot all about the hunger and thirst and weariness of that long day, and nestled her head into his neck, crooning with delight. Her tired little body relaxed, and she fell fast asleep, as she had been longing to do for the past three hours. Hamid, a little bent from the dead weight of her, wandered home along the river-path in the sweltering heat.

He rested for a while under a fig tree, watching the river where the women were washing their clothes and the cows cooled their feet. He wondered where the river went. One day he would find out for himself.

Once again, as night fell, the family gathered round the clay bowl and ate their supper by fire-light and candlelight. Kinza, refreshed from her sleep, sat on her mother's lap, flushed and bright-eyed, opening her mouth for food like a hungry baby bird. Hamid watched her, loving her, and remembering the pressure of her weary little body against his back. Always, always, he would protect her and make her happy.

The cows munched in the shed, and an old dog with a torn ear wandered in and lay down with his head on Rahma's lap. Moths and bats flitted in and out, and the cat crept up and stuck her head into the clay pot to have supper with the family.

Hamid, tired from his climb, lay down to sleep. He dreamt that the terrifying old beggar stood between him and Kinza. Suddenly he woke to find that the moon had risen and the grown-ups were still sitting talking round the dead charcoal.

In the silver beams he could see their faces clearly – his step-father grim and determined, Fatima cruelly pleased, and his mother pale and pleading.

"It is the only offer we shall ever get for her," said Si Mohamed fiercely. "She will be looked after for life."

"Life!" cried his mother bitterly, "there will be no life! She will die – she is so little and so weak..."

"A blind child is better dead!" remarked Fatima.

Zohra turned angrily on the old woman, but the man silenced them both by raising his hand.

"Silence, you foolish women!" he ordered. "Let there be no more talk about this. The child must come with me three days from now at dawn."

He rose grandly, like a king, and Fatima rose too. But Zohra stayed crouched by the dead fire, rocking herself to and fro in the moonlight.

"Little daughter! Little daughter!" she murmured brokenly to herself, and Hamid lay quite still and watched her. He dared not speak or go to her for fear of waking his step-father. But his hot little heart beat very fast, and his mind was completely made up.

"It shall not be!" he said to himself over and over again. "I will not let her go. It shall not be!"

He watched his mother creep away at last and

lie down sorrowfully to sleep. He watched the pale patch of moonlight move across the doorway and rest on the cradle where Kinza lay dreaming. He saw the pale summer dawn begin to break, and heard the first cock-crow – and all the time he lay thinking, thinking, thinking. But his thinking got him nowhere, and just before daybreak he fell into a deep sleep. Two hours later he was woken by his step-father prodding him with his foot.

"Wake up, you lazy creature!" growled Si Mohamed. "It's time you had the goats out."

Hamid rolled off his mattress, washed his face and hands in a bucket of water and started to eat his breakfast. Gobbling his bread and sipping his bowl of coffee, he glanced at his mother. Her face was pale, and there were dark circles under her eyes, but she did not look as unhappy as he had expected. There was a very determined expression on her face, as though she had made up her mind about something. Once Hamid found her staring hard at him, and he stared firmly back. She raised her eyebrows a little and he gave a slight nod. A secret understanding flashed between them. As soon as they could, they would talk together.

They did not have to wait very long. Hamid took the goats on to the hillside. With a crust of bread saved from his breakfast, he bribed a friend to watch them for him, then he crept back and watched through a gap in the hedge. Soon he saw his mother go across to where the grindstone stood, and after a few minutes he slipped in and joined her.

Kinza was sitting as usual with her face turned towards the eastern mountain, waiting for the sun to rise. Zohra sat cross-legged, turning the heavy wheel that crushed the corn.

Hamid crouched down beside her and touched her arm.

"Mother," he whispered, "I heard last night. Is it the old beggar who is having Kinza?"

His mother turned towards him, and her calm, steady gaze rested on him for a moment, as if she was making a decision. He was a thin little boy, small for his age, but very tough – and his love for Kinza was very strong.

"So my husband thinks," she replied, "but I say that it shall not be. I will not have Kinza starved in those cruel streets. No, Hamid, you must take her somewhere else. You can save her if you wish."

"Me!" echoed Hamid, amazed. But the look he gave his mother was reassuring – full of bravery and willing courage.

Chapter Five

Hamid agrees to help

"Listen," said Zohra, and Hamid's eyes never left her face as she spoke. All his life he would remember what she said to him that day.

"Four years ago," she said, "your father took me to the tomb across the mountains. We left you children with your grandmother, but I carried your little brother Absalom on my back, because he was only a baby. After we had visited the tomb, your father wanted to go on to the town further on. All day long we walked, from sunrise to sunset, in the burning heat. By the time we reached the town my feet were cut and blistered and Absalom was crying and feverish. His eyelids were swollen and stuck together, and he could not look at the light.

"Next morning, your father went off to the market to trade, but I sat holding my baby, shading his eyes from the light and brushing the flies off him.

"As I sat there, a woman from the town came up and began chatting to me, and she noticed the child.

'Your baby is sick?' she asked.

'Yes,' I replied, and turned his face so that she could see.

"She got up quickly. 'Come quick,' she said, 'there's an English nurse – she'll give you good medicine and heal your baby. She healed my little boy when he rubbed prickly pear thorns into his eyes.'

"I hung back. 'I have no money,' I said.

'It doesn't matter,' replied the woman. 'She is a holy woman, and heals without money because she loves her Saint. He is a good Saint, and has mercy on the poor.'

"'But,' I objected, 'the English are rich and live in grand houses. She will not receive me.'

"'But she lives in one of our houses,' answered the woman, 'and those who go to her for healing are mostly poor. None are ever turned away – I tell you, she receives them in the name of her Saint.'

"So I followed, feeling afraid, but eager for medicine that would cure my baby's eyes. She led me down a narrow back street to a house with an open door. There were people coming out of that door – poor people like me, with babies tied on their backs. Some of them carried bottles of medicine and none of them looked afraid.

"We were only just in time, for the room was nearly empty. The nurse was tall and fair. I had never seen anyone like her before. She spoke kindly to everyone, and I saw her take little children up in her arms as though she loved them. As I watched her, my fear went away, and when everyone else had gone I went up to her and held out Absalom. She took him in her lap and examined his eyes. Her hands were very gentle. He didn't even cry.

"She asked me many questions about him, and then she gave me medicine for his fever and ointment for his eyes. While she fetched them I looked at a picture on the wall. It was the picture of a man with a kind face, holding a little child in his arms, and lots of other little children clinging to his robe, looking up at him.

"I asked her who that man was, and she said he was called Jesus, and he was sent from God to show us the way to Heaven. She told me a lot about him, how he healed the sick, and made blind people see, and loved everyone, whether they were rich or poor, grown-ups or children. I know she loved the man in the picture and wanted to be like him – and that was why she gave me medicine and was kind to Absalom."

Zohra paused, and then went on speaking very slowly.

"And I think for the sake of the man in the picture, she would shelter Kinza, and so you must carry Kinza to her. You must start tonight when the moon is full, and you must walk all night and hide by day, for Si Mohamed will certainly search for you.

"But he need not know you are gone till tomorrow night. I will send Rahma out early with the goats before he's awake, and tell him you've taken them. He never bothers to look at Kinza in any case, and I'll put a pillow in her cradle in case

Fatima glances in. By the time he comes home from work it will be dusk and he cannot send out a search by night, nor will I tell him where you've gone. By the next day, you will be nearly there."

Hamid's eyes were bright with fear and excitement, but he only said "How shall I know the way?"

"I've thought of that," replied his mother, "and there is only one road you can take. You must follow the river to the top of the valley and then you must climb the mountain. It is very high, but you must reach the top. Below you will see another river in a valley, and if you follow the road along the bank, you will at last reach a big main road with traffic. If you start walking up this road, it may be that a lorry driver will give you a ride, for the town lies about 50 kilometres along it up in the mountains. If you cannot get a ride you must walk it, and may God help you."

"And when I get there?" breathed the little boy.

"When you get there," said his mother, "you must find the house of the English nurse. Do not ask, but just watch. She lives in a street behind the market and opposite the doorway of the inn. Her house is the last one in the street. Go to her, tell her all our story, and give her Kinza. She will know what to do next."

Hamid looked doubtful. "But what if she doesn't want Kinza?" he asked.

His mother shook her head. "She won't turn her away," she replied confidently. "She told me her Saint in the picture never turned anyone away. For the sake of her Saint I know she will receive her and be good to her. Now, you must go back to your goats, and I must finish the grinding, or Fatima will be angry. Think about what I have told you, and I'll bake extra loaves of bread for you to carry on your journey."

Hamid got up to go back to his goats, feeling like someone in a dream. The world was really just the same as it had been yesterday, but to the eyes of the little boy it seemed different. Yet in spite of his fear about the journey, he never thought of refusing to go.

He whistled softly and a few young goats grazing nearby came up and pushed their noses into his lap. He suddenly knew he loved them, and would be sorry to leave them. He wondered when he would see them again, and for the first time he began to think about his own future, as well as Kinza's. He certainly could not come back for a long time. His step-father would be much too angry.

He led them home early that evening and sat quietly down beside his mother and Rahma, who were busy spinning wool. Both were working hard because Fatima was sitting by watching, and neither spoke when Hamid joined them.

Hamid's young heart ached. Except when his mother had gone on five days' pilgrimage to the tomb, he had never spent a night in his life away from her. Now he must leave her for a long time. Her silent love flowed out to him, comforting and strengthening him.

The evening dragged on and the light faded. Tonight everything felt different. For the first time in his life Hamid was not hungry when the family gathered round the supper bowl, but he forced himself to eat in case Si Mohamed should notice. Then without a word he went out and lay down by the door and waited, battling with his fears and thoughts until his step-father had fallen asleep, and the moon had risen.

He watched his step-father lie down at last, and listened until his breathing became heavy and regular. Yes, he was sleeping deeply, snoring in his dreams. Only a little longer now. Hamid crept to the edge of the mattress and waited, with his eyes fixed on the mountain. On silent feet he stepped through the doorway and slipped behind the granary.

The old dog cocked his ear and rattled its chain, and Hamid held his breath. If the dog should bark the whole plan would be ruined. He flung himself down beside it, burying his face in its mangy coat, fondling its ears and wordlessly begging it to be silent. It turned its large head and licked the child's face, puzzled but loyal.

So he crouched waiting, with his arms round the dog's neck, listening for his mother. He jumped as she appeared, with Kinza in her arms.

In complete silence she tied Kinza to his back. The baby wondered what was happening, but, trusting them completely, she laid her head down on her brother's shoulder and fell fast asleep again. Then Zohra tied two loaves of bread on his other shoulder, took both his hands in hers and kissed them. He in turn pressed her fingers to his lips and clung to her for a moment. Then she gently sent him on his way and stood watching as he passed through the gate. Not a word had passed between them. Then, content with what she had done, she went back to her hut – to the empty cradle and the anger of her husband. And Hamid, like a small boat cut loose from its moorings and swept out into unknown seas, set off along the moonlit path.

Chapter Six

Adventures on the way

Uphill, downhill, along the river path, Hamid trudged on, becoming more and more exhausted. Kinza seemed to weigh heavier and heavier on his back. He remembered all he had left behind – his mother, Rahma, the thatched hut and charcoal fire, the goats and the dog with the torn ear. He felt afraid of the unknown he was walking towards, but he knew he must keep going.

At last, exhausted, he reached a cornfield, and, hiding himself and Kinza amongst the tall stalks, they fell asleep. Kinza woke before Hamid and, crawling out from the prickly cornstalks, she started to explore. She heard the sound of a grindstone, and with a cry of delight, she staggered towards it. Grindstones meant mother – and food and shelter and comfort.

A woman sitting at the door of her hut heard the cry and looked up. She could hardly believe her eyes! Staggering towards her was the strangest little figure she had ever seen – a tiny child in a cotton gown, her outstretched hands groping, her face lifted to the light. Her black, tangled curls had straw sticking out all over them like a halo.

Kinza realised she was in a strange place, and hesitated for a moment. Then she held her arms out and cried "Mummy!"

The woman sitting at the grindstone was a young woman whose only child had died six months ago. Now, this baby staggered towards her crying the very word she had been longing to hear. She lifted Kinza into her lap, and began kissing and soothing her.

Kinza knew this was not her mother, and started to struggle free, but although these were the wrong arms, they felt safe and strong, and the woman's hands were gentle as they stroked her curls. At last she relaxed and asked for a drink. The woman fetched her a bowl of buttermilk. She drank every last drop, then curled up like a kitten in the woman's lap and went to sleep.

It was evening when Hamid woke up, feeling rested and comfortable. He suddenly realised where he was and jumped up with a little cry of alarm. Where was Kinza? He saw her tracks in the trampled corn and crept to the edge of the patch. What he saw gave him a real surprise.

Less than fifty yards away he saw Kinza eating cherries in front of a hut, while a young woman laughed and tried to untangle her curls. Around them sat the whole village, who had come out to stare at this strange child who had somehow arrived amongst them.

Hamid felt ashamed. He had fallen asleep, they had lost a whole precious day's travelling, and, worst of all, Kinza had escaped and could well be in an enemy camp. He must rescue her quickly, for these people would certainly soon come to hear of the child missing from Thursday village.

So, once again when the sun went down and moonlight flooded the village, Hamid left the shelter of the cornfield and crept over to the doorway of the hut. Kinza had been put on a little mat, covered with a goatskin. Hamid scooped her up in his arms, whispering her name. She gave a little sigh and half woke but, knowing she was safely back with her brother, she clung to him tightly and fell into a deep, peaceful sleep. She knew she was back in the right place.

Five minutes later they were bumping up the hillside, Hamid's heart thumping with fear. But no one had heard them – the rescue had been perfect.

Hamid paused and looked up to the mountain towering above him, and back to the valley and the river that led home. He knew which path he had to take, and headed towards the mountain top, which he reached just before dawn. Hamid felt he was standing alone on top of the world, gazing at range upon range of rocky peaks.

He knew he had to avoid Tuesday Market, a Spanish settlement where there were many soldiers who might be on the look-out for them. His stepfather could well have alerted the police by now. Hamid knew he must make his way straight down the mountain to the river in the valley two thousand feet below them.

He tied Kinza on his back again and set out, almost colliding with two men on horseback, whom he recognised as coming from his own village.

Dazzled by the sun, the men stared at him for a moment, then one leaped lightly from his horse and made a grab for Hamid.

"It's Si Mohamed's boy!" he cried. "The one who was missing from Thursday Market the day before yesterday."

Hamid ducked and bolted down the mountainside. His sudden movement startled the horse, which reared in the air. The man gave an angry shout and the horse plunged forward. By the time the animal was properly under control, Hamid was far away, leaping through the scrub, with Kinza bumping behind him. Not even noticing the thorns and roots and his cut, bleeding feet, he went crashing on, not daring to look behind, always expecting a heavy hand to land on his shoulder and pull Kinza away from him.

The merchant, still clinging to the bridle, stood watching him. He had done his best, but he was not going to chase someone else's brat all over the scrub bushes and spoil his new shoes. It was none of his business, and he wanted to be in good time for market. He shrugged his shoulders, mounted his horse and rode on. He would tell the police at Tuesday Market. It was their job, not his, to hunt runaway boys.

But poor Hamid dared not stop running, and Kinza, with her body nearly shaken to bits, gave jerky wails and hiccups on his back. There seemed to be nowhere to hide. Once he caught his foot in a root and fell headlong. Bruised and dirty, he was up in a second, but he had noticed a rock jutting out ahead of him. He made for it blindly, rounded it, and found himself close to a thatched hut, and beside the hut was a mud goat-shed.

Hamid was quite certain that his enemy would appear at any minute round the rock, and this was his very last hope of escape.

He sprang into the close dark shelter of the goat-shed, and found a sick goat and her kid lying on some straw. There was a pile of hay stacked against the wall, and Hamid burrowed into it. Then, like a hunted rabbit, he lay panting and shivering for half an hour.

When his heart was beating more normally, he wriggled himself round in the straw and began to think about his situation. He felt very ill; he was burning hot, and his head ached dreadfully. His limbs were heavy and stiff, and the straw pricked and rubbed his bleeding feet.

They had had nothing to drink that morning, and his mouth was parched with fear and running. Kinza too was miserable, and wanted a drink. She had started to cry, sounding like a starved kitten, and he could not silence her. If anyone came to the shed, they would certainly hear her.

He looked around desperately, and then for the first time he began to consider the sick goat, which had broken its front leg. He cheered up at once, for here was the answer to his problems. Hamid understood goats, and a mother with a kid would have plenty of milk.

He wormed his way out of the hay, and, creeping

to the doorway, grabbed hold of a piece of broken clay pot that had been thrown away. Then, with one eye on the house, he made friends with the goat and the kid, fondling their ears and letting them lick his hands. Then, once she trusted him, he lay down on the floor beside the mother and milked it into the piece of pot. He carried the sweet, warm, frothing milk to Kinza, who drank it all up and mewed for more. They drank as much as they could, and soaked hard pieces of bread into it, for they were parched and starving.

The excitement of milking, the pain in his feet, the stuffy heat of the straw pile and the fever in his own body had kept Hamid awake all morning. He was terrified of going to sleep, too, in case Kinza wandered off again. He looked round for a piece of rope to tie her to him, but there was nothing suitable, and he dared not go out until it was dark. At last, exhausted, he clasped her tightly to him and fell into a deep sleep.

But Kinza, realising he was asleep, and wanting to do just as she pleased, crawled out of the pile of hay. She took a few uncertain steps and bumped straight into the goat.

Kinza loved goats and felt perfectly at home with them, so having found what she wanted – friendly company and a place to lie in which did not scratch – she crawled under the goat's chin and curled up to sleep. The little kid, no doubt feeling jealous, butted its way in, so they lay together with the goat's front legs around them, both quite content – the new-born kid and the lost baby.

Hamid, turning feverishly in his sleep, soon tossed away the straw and lay with his arms and face exposed. Towards sunset, the mother of the household came in with a bucket to milk the lame goat. For a moment she thought it had had another kid – then she looked more closely and found it was a little girl curled up in a ball.

"May God have mercy on me!" exclaimed the woman. "It's a baby!"

She looked around, puzzled, and caught sight of Hamid's top half sticking out of the straw.

"May God have mercy on my parents!" she cried out. "There's a boy as well!"

She marched quickly over to him and prodded him with her leathery foot. She was a big woman, with a loud voice, and she wanted an explanation quickly.

Hamid woke with a start and struggled into a sitting position. He was fuzzy with sleep, but realised at once that wherever he was he was cornered and caught like a rat in a trap. His head still ached terribly, and he lost all control of himself. He stuffed his knuckles into his eyes and began to cry.

"Stop it!" said the woman, slapping him on the back. "You are not from our village. Who are you? And where have you come from?"

Hamid gulped back his sobs, and looked at her. He thought it might be best to tell the truth, and the woman listened to his story, frowning and nodding in turn.

When he had finished she looked at him kindly. It was a good story and seemed true enough. She had been married twice, and her first husband had been very cruel to her and her child. He had divorced her when she was only fifteen years old. She too had known what it was to see her baby ill-treated, and she felt sorry for this unknown woman who was willing to risk so much for her blind child.

Besides all this, the woman had a motherly heart, and the bright-eyed boy who coughed as he spoke was obviously ill. She knew nothing yet about the filthy little bundle cuddling her goat, but at least she could give her a better spot to sleep in. So she milked her goat, and then, with the bucket in her right hand and Kinza under her left arm, she strode to her house, with Hamid limping behind her.

The house was a round mud-hut, rather dark inside, with a stack of winter bedding for the goats heaped against the wall. A clay pot bubbled on a fire, and three little girls sat around it expectantly. As they entered, the husband came down the mountain-side with the flock, and they all gathered round to eat. Hamid, who had eaten nothing but bread and milk for two days, thought he had never tasted anything so good – a lentil stew, flavoured with garlic, oil and red peppers with hunks of hot, soft bread to dip in it; a bowl of buttermilk from which they all drank in turn; and finally a dish of bruised apricots – the unbruised ones the father would carry to the Wednesday Market at dawn next day.

Hamid felt his strength come back to him. For one night at least he would be safe and sheltered, and this made him feel peaceful and his head stopped aching. The big countrywoman sat licking her fingers, and he gazed up at her as though she was an angel from heaven.

After supper the three little girls curled themselves up on goatskins against the hay, with a cat and her three kittens for company, and went straight to sleep. The father went out to milk, and his wife followed because she wanted to talk to him. Hamid, sitting by the fire with Kinza leaning up against him, could hear their voices. He supposed they were talking about him, and he was quite right, for the woman came back soon with everything fixed up.

"Don't be afraid," she said encouragingly, "my husband is quite willing to help you. He is going into Wednesday Market tomorrow to sell apricots. He picks up a lorry at the bottom of the hill just before daybreak. He will take you with him and say you are my sister's children, for my sister lives on the road to Friday Market, where you are trying to get to, and she has a boy about your age and a baby girl. The lorry will drop you about twenty-five kilometres from Friday Market, on the main road, and you can probably get a lift – if not, it's not too far to walk."

She looked down at his joyful face and suddenly felt sorry because he was so young and helpless. She fetched a basin and a towel and, stooping down, she washed his bruised, cut feet. Then she tore a rag into strips and bathed his wounds with olive oil. Finally, she laid him on one sheepskin with his little sister, and covered them warmly with another. He fell asleep at once, grateful and unafraid, and she went and sat very still on her doorstep, her hands folded, looking out into the dusk.

Chapter Seven

Hamid completes his mission

Twenty-four hours later Hamid found himself gazing up at the walls of the city he had come so far to find, feeling more strange and lost than he had ever felt before in his life.

He had had a very successful day. He had woken at cock-crow, cool and refreshed. The woman had fed them and blessed them, and sent them out with her husband. At the bottom of the hill a lorry, jammed tight with market-goers, had picked them up and rattled off down the valley. Hamid had never been in a lorry before and the noise and speed and jolting thrilled him. The main road thrilled him, too, with its roaring traffic, and the two hours' drive passed all too quickly. The road turned off to Wednesday Market, and he and Kinza were dropped about twenty-five kilometres from their destination.

He had walked all day, patiently plodding along in the heat, often sitting down to rest. At one point he decided to stop and wash out Kinza's little dress in the river as he thought that nobody was going to be really pleased to see her unless she was a little bit cleaner. When she was redressed, he decided she looked fit for a palace.

He had climbed a long, long hill, stopping to pick wild flowers along the way for Kinza to present to her new mother. At last he rounded a bend in the road and just ahead of him was the old city wall and the town inside, in the shadow of the bare jagged mountains.

Hamid stood in the cool of the shadow of the gate, and watched for a while. He did not think he would have to ask the way if he could find the market, for his mother had described the house exactly, and he was afraid to speak to anyone. He thought he would wait until night-time before making his way along those narrow, crowded, cobbled streets. It would be easier to slip along in the dark. But as dusk deepened he saw the shop-keepers on each side of the streets turn on the lights, and everyone walked past in the full glare of them. Apparently in this terrifying place there was no darkness and no hiding. The sooner he could safely get rid of Kinza the better.

He set off timidly along the cobbles, marvelling at the beautiful things displayed in the shops – the bright silks, piles of fruit and stacks of bread. It seemed to him like fairyland, and he gazed, bright-eyed and fascinated, at all this beauty – a magic town where everything glittered and dazzled. He forgot that he had felt lonely and afraid, and gazed up eagerly into the faces of the shop-keepers and passers-by. But no one smiled at him or looked kindly at him, and no one welcomed him to the golden city.

He crept along until he came to a splashing fountain where a little girl was filling buckets. She at least looked a kind little girl and very shyly he asked her the way to the inn above the market. She pointed him in the right direction.

It was not far. The old archway leading into the inn courtyard stood back from the street. Weary mules and donkeys were passing in and travellers stood in groups looking out on the market. Hamid longed to go and rest on the straw with the donkeys, but he had no coin to pay for such shelter, and anyway, he felt his business had better be done that night.

He thought the house of the nurse would not be difficult to find, and he set off confidently. The street curved and he stopped. He could see the end now, and the rubbish tip beyond, and what he saw filled him with surprise.

There was a dim street-lamp outside the last house on the left, and under it he could see a group of little boys, dirty and ragged like himself, standing as if they were waiting for something to happen. As Hamid watched, the door was opened from the inside and a beam of bright light shone out on to the cobbles. The children surged forwards, tumbling over each other, and disappeared through the golden doorway. Then he heard other footsteps behind him, and three more little boys in black tatters rushed past him on swift, bare feet. They too went in. Then, as Hamid stood still in the shadows he heard the sound of singing, and he thought he had never heard anything so beautiful.

Lured by the music he crept closer, skulking along the wall, and at last he reached the top of the step and dared to peep in. Then he gasped with joy and excitement, for he was looking across a passageway into another room, and hanging on the wall of that room exactly opposite the doorway was the picture of the man who loved little children, carrying in his arms a curly-haired baby just about Kinza's age. Boys and girls were crowding round him, holding out their arms, and he smiled down on them and did not seem to want them to go away. Hamid remembered the hard faces of the shop-keepers – this man was unlike any of them. He would certainly welcome Kinza just as he was welcoming the crowd of happy children in the picture.

But who were all those ragged little boys? And why did they go in? And what were they singing about? He could not see them, for they all gathered at one end of the room, but he could hear a woman's voice. As he listened, crouching on the step, straining to catch the words, the children began to chant something all together, as though they were learning it by heart, just as they did in the mosque schools when they learned the Koran.

"Jesus said 'I am the light of the world; he that follows me shall not walk in darkness, but shall have the light of life.'"

What could it mean?

Three times they repeated the verse and Hamid whispered the words with them, and tucked them away in his memory to think about afterwards.

The immediate problem now was, what to do about Kinza?

If all these children belonged to the nurse, she would certainly not want another. No little girls had gone into the house, so perhaps the English, like his own people, on the whole preferred boys. Kinza's chances seemed very small if he knocked on the door and presented her as a gift. He must think of a better way than that.

Then he thought of a plan which he was certain would work because his mother had said that the Saint in the picture had never been known to turn a child away. He would simply leave Kinza in the passage, like a surprise parcel, to explain herself as best as she could. If this nurse was really like her Saint, she would not throw such a tiny helpless creature homeless into the street on a dark night.

He skipped across the orange beam of light and sat down on the rubbish heap. He shook Kinza until she was thoroughly wide awake and then spoke to her very solemnly.

"Kinza, little sister," he said, "I am going to sit you down by yourself, and you must keep very still and not cry. If you cry, a lady will beat you hard. If you don't cry she will soon come and give you a nice sweet."

Now Kinza understood this perfectly. She knew all about being hit if she did not keep still, and she seldom got what she wanted by crying. Also, she was very hungry. So she let Hamid smooth and pat her and then, placing the withered bunch of flowers in her hand, he crept off the rubbish heap. He pushed the door open a little way, lifted Kinza over the step, and sat her down in the dark passage.

Hamid suddenly felt his throat tighten and his eyes fill with tears. Kinza would never be his own again, and he realised how much he loved her. As a sign of his love, he took out his last dry crust from the cloth and thrust it into her hand. Then he left her sitting cross-legged against the wall, very tousled and very crumpled, clasping a bunch of dead poppies and an old crust, for the surprise and delight of the missionary lady.

But through the blur of his tears he had caught sight once again of the face of the man in the picture, and he seemed to be smiling straight at Kinza. Hamid felt comforted. Then, crouching against the wall of a little alley leading off the street, he tried to remember the words he had heard three times over: "Jesus said 'I am the light of the world ... instead of darkness you can have the light of life.'" It was something like that, and whatever could it mean?

What was the light of the world? He thought of the lamp burning in his hut at home and the flickering shadows on the wall. He remembered the moonlit journey, and the circling stars, and the sunrise on top of the mountain. Moonlight, starlight, sunlight, candlelight, and the orange glare of the city street – they had all faded now. He was sitting alone in a very dark alley, and the moon had not yet risen behind the wall of rock. But Jesus said that instead of darkness you can have the light of life. "I am the light of the world." He thought of Kinza, always living in darkness – could this light which he had never seen ever reach her? What did it all mean? If only it wasn't so dark... if only he wasn't so hungry... if only he could have kept Kinza... if only he could run home to his mother.

He stopped short in his thoughts, and leaned forward eagerly. A crowd of boys came hurrying down the street, and at the corner they turned and waved. They were talking excitedly, all at once, so Hamid could not hear very well what they said, but he caught odd words: "Who is she?" – "Such a little girl!" – "Where is her mother?" Then the boys passed out of sight, and the street was left in silence.

Then, because he was longing to know what had happened, he tiptoed out of his alley and prowled back to the rubbish heap. The door through which he had posted Kinza was fast shut, and no sound came from inside. What had happened? There was a light in an upper window, and Hamid crossed the street and stood with his back pressed against the wall of the house opposite, gazing upwards. As he stood there looking, there passed across the lighted window the figure of a woman nestling a little child in her arms, and the child showed no sign of fear. It neither struggled nor cried. It lay at peace with one little hand uplifted to feel the face bowed over it.

Hamid had successfully completed his mission. All was well with Kinza. Not knowing where else to go, he slunk back to the rubbish heap, and covering himself as best he could with his rags, he curled up against the wall to sleep, with his head resting on his arm.

Chapter Eight

Doughnuts and street-boys

Hamid woke early next morning, stiff and cold, and blamed himself for wanting to sleep so near the house. Yet somehow it comforted him to know that Kinza was close to him. He wondered whether she had woken yet, and what she was doing. He wandered along the street and out into the deserted market, wondering what to do, where to go, and above all where his breakfast would come from. He was sure that Kinza was eating well, and rather regretted having given her that last crust.

It looked a golden city no longer. The shops were shuttered, and a few homeless beggars lay up against the temple steps, still fast asleep. Now his mission was completed, Hamid felt horribly flat and tired, and he stood in the middle of the market longing for home.

Then he heard a familiar sound – the harsh rattle of a stork's cry and the rush of great wings as they swooped over him, just as they used to do when he was with his goats on his own mountain. He looked up quickly and saw her flying up high to her nest in the turret of an old fort. He stared at the massive old walls and found that he was standing opposite an old gate in an archway leading into a garden.

The gate was wide open and there seemed no one to stop him. Hamid trotted across the cobbles, climbed the steps and tip-toed through. He found himself standing in the most beautiful garden he had ever seen in his life. It was square in shape, and in the middle was a fountain surrounded by green lawns and colourful flower-beds. But while he was enjoying it all, a keeper came through the archway and ordered him out.

The town was beginning to wake up now, and Hamid found himself standing with his back to a little stall where a man was frying doughnuts in a deep stone trough of oil. He was obviously busy, having to do everything himself, and this had put him in a bad temper, for he was muttering and growling to himself.

Hamid suddenly had an idea. Drawing as near as he could to that delicious smell, and being desperate with hunger, he boldly walked up to the man and asked him if he needed an assistant.

The man looked him up and down. His usual boy had not turned up that morning, and Sillam, the doughnut-maker, was prepared to accept help from the first boy who came along. He opened the wooden barrier and beckoned Hamid inside.

He did not recognise him, and did not know whether or not he was a thief.

"Take the bellows," he said, "and blow up this fire, and if I find you helping yourself to anything that doesn't belong to you, the police station is opposite!"

Hamid squatted down and began to blow. He did not feel very well; it was so hot, and the leaping flames scorched his face. Many little boys before him had been unable to stand the heat. At last he heard his master's voice say "Enough," and he staggered to his feet, dizzy and flushed.

"Now stand there and thread the doughnuts on to the blades of grass," said Sillam. Hamid worked quickly enough, burning his fingers a little, but not minding much because he was too hungry to think about anything else except the pains inside him. But he did notice that quite a crowd of tattered, grimy little boys were watching him closely. He realised that somehow, before long, he would have to say who he was.

He had worked for about two hours when the master suddenly said, "Have you had any breakfast?"

"No," said Hamid, "and no supper last night, either."

Sillam handed him a couple of hot, golden doughnuts. With a sigh of relief Hamid bit into the first one. It was wonderful. But the dark eyes of the little boys watching him suddenly became hostile. They were hungry, too, and this stranger was taking a job they wanted.

Doughnuts are a breakfast food, and the shop shut at mid-morning. The master told Hamid he had worked well, and could return early next day. Then he gave him a small coin, and Hamid, feeling like a king, strutted across the market to decide how to spend it. He noticed a pile of sticky green sweets, and longed to buy one for Kinza. But Kinza probably no longer needed green sweets. Perhaps she had forgotten all about him already. He suddenly felt sad, and decided to stop thinking about it, and turn his attention to the baker's shop.

A voice at his side suddenly said, "Who are you?" and he turned to see a little boy about his own age, with a shaved, spotted head, dressed in a dirty white gown. A strange little figure, but his dark eyes were bright and intelligent, and he looked at Hamid in quite a friendly way.

Hamid faced him shyly. "I'm from the country," he replied.

"Why have you come to town?"

"To find work."

"Where are your mother and father?"

"Dead."

"Where do you live?"

"In the street."

The little boy, whose name was Ayashi, nodded approvingly. "I too," he said cheerfully, "have no mother, and my father has gone to the mountains. I too live in the streets. We all do. Now, buy us a loaf with the money the master gave you, and give us each a piece. Then you shall be one of us and we will show you where we go for supper at night."

His confident voice and cheerful acceptance of his homelessness fascinated Hamid. "You shall be one of us" were wonderful words. Hamid bought his loaf quickly and spent the change on a handful of black, bitter olives. Then he followed his new friend to the eucalyptus tree in the middle of the square, where the gang squatted in the shade. He handed over the food to be divided up, and they fell upon it eagerly.

Hamid, with his portion, sat a little apart through shyness, but although no one said "Thank you," the gift had done its work. From that day onwards he was truly one of them.

It was a strange gang which he joined that day – they were all dirty, ignorant and poor, dressed in rags and tatters; children who had never been loved. Tough and hardy they were, crafty and quick through living by their wits. Thieving, lying and swearing were regular habits, yet they made the most of their pleasures. Hamid, watching silently, felt so proud to be sitting amongst them. He had never met boys like these, and he thought they were wonderful – so tough and manly, easy-going and independent. He longed to become like them, and he wriggled nearer.

He realised that they earned their livings in lots of different ways. Some worked on looms certain days a week, and others, like himself, helped in the doughnut shops. They all begged in between, and hung around the hotel on the off-chance of carrying a bag for a tourist or watching a car. Some slept with their families at night in hovels they called home, while others crept into the mosques. Life was uncertain and exciting, and there seemed only one sure thing in the day – and that was their supper at the home of the English nurse.

Now they were all discussing the extraordinary things that had happened the night before. None of them had ever seen the strange little girl before, they said. No one knew where she came from. She held up her arms to the English nurse and called for her mother, but she would not say anything else. So the nurse had picked her up and taken her in, and today she was going to look for the baby's parents.

"And what if she doesn't find them?" asked one little boy. "Will she put her out in the street?"

Ayashi looked up quickly. "She will not," he replied with complete confidence.

"How do you know? Why not? It is not her child!" exclaimed the other children all together.

"Because," answered Ayashi simply, "she has a clean heart."

Chapter Nine

Supper at the nurse's home

The rest of the day passed pleasantly. Ayashi, pleased by Hamid's admiration, took him round the town and up on to the hillside to show him the spring of water welling up from the heart of the mountain. It never failed, and kept the city supplied and the fields around it fresh and green.

At mid-day they hung round the door of the hotel. After a time a waiter flung them some broken rolls and meat that guests had left on their plates, and the boys fell upon them like hungry dogs. Then they curled themselves against the trunk of the eucalyptus tree and slept in the shade.

Evening came, and Hamid stuck close to Ayashi. They sat on some steps together with a few friends, watching the country people crowding into the square. Tomorrow was market day, and those who had come from a distance would spread out their sacks against the wall and sleep beside their wares. As darkness fell the shop-keepers lit their lamps again, and other little boys sauntered up from their various jobs and collected on the steps.

"Come," said Ayashi, who seemed to be a sort of leader among them, "she will soon open her door now."

He beckoned Hamid to follow him, but Hamid hesitated. He felt torn in two; hunger and his great longing to see whether all was well with his little sister urged him on, but caution held him back. What if he should be forced to speak while Kinza was there? She would certainly recognise his voice and run to him, and then everyone would be suspicious.

"Come on," called Ayashi impatiently, looking back.

Hamid shook his head. "I'm not coming," he replied, and sat down again on the steps, with his head in his hands, staring gloomily into the market. Then he got up suddenly, for he had had an idea. He would not go in, but he would creep to the door of the house, as he had done the night before, and peep through a crack. Perhaps he would catch a glimpse of Kinza.

Like some guilty little thief, he darted into the quiet back street and sneaked along the wall towards the open door.

He peered round very cautiously, but there was no sign or sound of her – only the murmuring of voices, and then the shrill noise of the little boys singing. Kinza was apparently nowhere about, and he was standing in a very dangerous position.

He shuffled on to the rubbish heap, and began to cry quietly because his friends and his little sister were all inside the house where there was shelter and light and food – and he was left outside.

And then something happened. The door opened a little farther, and the nurse stepped out into the street to see if any more boys were coming before she started the lesson. She appeared silently, and Hamid did not see her at first. But she heard a wretched, sniffing sound close by and, looking round, she spotted him on the rubbish heap.

Hamid jumped up, frightened, but she stood between him and freedom and he could not escape, so he rubbed away his tears and crouched staring up at her. He had never seen anyone like her before.

"Why don't you come in?" she asked.

Attracted by a sense of welcome, he got up and walked slowly towards her. She waited quite still, afraid of startling him. Then, when he was close to her, she held out her hand. He took it and stepped trustfully through the doorway with her.

They entered the lighted room together, and Hamid took a good look round. It was a long white-washed room, with a rush mat on the floor and mattresses against the wall. At one end the boys sat cross-legged in a semicircle. On the wall opposite the door was the picture of the Saint smiling down on them, just as he had smiled down on Kinza.

"Come," said the nurse, "sit down with the others. I'm going to show you something."

Ayashi grinned at him delightedly, and Hamid wormed his way into the semicircle and sat beside him. The boys looked younger here somehow, not like men of the world any more.

The nurse sat down on the mattress in front of them and showed them a little book. It was quite unlike the Koran, which was the only book Hamid had ever seen inside. None of the boys could read at all, anyway.

Their teacher explained how God lived in a place like a bright golden city – heaven – where there were only good things, and happiness.

I'd like to go there, thought Hamid, it would be even better than our village – no fear, no quarrelling, no blindness.

But while he was thinking about this wonderful place the nurse told them that because of the bad things people do wrong, God cannot let them into the city. The gate is shut to wrong-doers. Hamid had never worried about doing wrong before – in fact, he had never even thought about what wrong was. Of course he stole if he got the chance, and naturally he told lies if they would save him from a beating – why shouldn't he?

Then the nurse went on to tell them a strange story. Apparently, God's son, whose name was Jesus, had left this wonderful city and come down into the world to live with the people he loved. At the end, he had died, on a cross, as a punishment for all the wrong things everybody has ever done. He had done nothing wrong himself, and didn't deserve to die, but because he loved people so much, he wanted them to be able to go and live in his home – heaven – with him. He had died in place of everyone else – even bad, lying, thieving little boys like Hamid and the rest of the gang. All they had to do was say sorry, and ask Jesus to forgive them.

Then the nurse stopped talking and brought in two great bowls of steaming rice and handed round hunks of bread. The children divided up into two groups and huddled over their supper, scooping up the food at an amazing pace, then polishing the bowls with their dirty little fingers. No one spoke much until the last lick and crumb had vanished because they were racing each other to get the most. When every bit had gone, they sat back on their heels and questioned the nurse about the little girl whom they had found in the passage the night before.

"She is still with me," she said, smiling a little. "She is, at this moment, asleep in bed."

Hamid looked at her hard. She did not seem to be annoyed at Kinza still being with her.

"I have taken her all round the town with me today," went on the nurse, "but nobody has ever seen her before, or knows who her parents are. She is a little blind girl, so I suppose no one wants her."

"And what will you do with her?" asked the boys, all together.

"Well, I shall have to keep her for the moment; there's nothing else to be done." This time she laughed outright, and Hamid nearly laughed too, with joy and relief. He had a wild, reckless longing to see his little sister asleep in bed, and he was no longer afraid. He waited until the little boys had bowed and shaken hands with their hostess, and skipped off into the dark. Then she turned and found him lingering in the passage. His heart was beating violently, but he spoke steadily and boldly.

"I come from a village," he said, "and in my village there are two or three blind baby girls whose parents come into the market. Let me see her, and perhaps I can tell you who her mother is."

The nurse looked down at him, surprised. She had certainly never seen this little boy before, and he might be speaking the truth. She had watched him since he had entered her house, and noticed his thin, tired face and his bruised feet – also the ravenous way he had fallen on his food. She guessed he had travelled a long way, and was glad to shelter him, so she led him to a room upstairs, where Kinza lay on a mattress, fast asleep.

She looked different because she had had a bath and had come out quite another colour. Also her hair had been washed and cut, and instead of her tangles she had soft, dark curls falling over her forehead. Her old dress had been changed for a little white night-dress, spotlessly clean. Hamid gazed at her, fascinated, for a while, and then looked round the room. It was brightly lit, and furnished simply, but there were pretty covers on the mattresses, books on the shelves and pictures on the walls. He longed to stay with her, but knew it was not possible.

"I do not know her," he said gravely. "She is not one of the children from our village."

He followed the nurse downstairs in silence, and she came to the door and let him out. He stepped into the street, looked up into her face and took hold of the hand that had been so kind to Kinza.

"You are good!" he said simply. "Your food is good; your teaching is good; your heart is good. May God have mercy on your ancestors!"

Then he bounded away down the street and disappeared into the darkness.

Chapter Ten

Hamid learns a lesson for life

Hamid kept his job at the doughnut shop. He worked hard, and his master was usually quite kind to him, giving him his breakfast and his coin regularly. The coin he spent on dinner, and the nurse provided him with his supper. He slept with Ayashi just inside the mosque, and as long as the sun shone and the weather kept warm he was happy. There was always plenty to do. They helped with the harvesting, and picked olives. On hot days they went bathing in the rocky stream that flowed from the spring in the mountain and washed all their dirt away.

Five days a week they went to the house of the English nurse. Hamid knew many stories about Jesus now. He knew that he was not a saint at all, but the Son of God who had come down into this world. He knew that the lame and the blind had come to Jesus, and he had healed them. Hamid wished that he also had lived then, for he would have carried Kinza to him, and her eyes would have been opened. He knew that Jesus had died with his arms stretched out in welcome on a cross and he had been placed in a rock tomb. He had come to life again and left the tomb. Then he had been seen in a beautiful garden.

He knew too that Jesus had gone back to heaven, the City of Light, and was still alive, and that the living Spirit of Jesus was willing to come into the hearts of people, to make them good.

Summer drew into autumn, and the nights became colder and longer. There were no more tourists in the hotel now, so there were no cars to watch and no luggage to carry. The boys often begged for money or scraps at rich people's houses. Life became hard and uncertain. The only comfort that could really be depended on was supper at the house of the English nurse.

She lit a charcoal fire for them these nights, and let them in early. They would troop across her hall, leaving a trail of black footprints on the tiles, their rags dripping. Then they would huddle round the glowing coals to warm their blue fingers, and gradually their teeth would stop chattering.

Clothes were a great problem just now. The wind and rain pierced and rotted their rags, and Hamid wondered just how much longer his flimsy summer gown would hold together. He did not know what he would do when it finally fell to pieces. Some of his friends had begged or stolen sacks, but Hamid had not been lucky.

Kinza, on the other hand, had no clothes

problem. She always went shopping with the English nurse, and Hamid often saw her waddling across the market on legs that had grown amazingly fat and sturdy during the past two months. Over her clean gown she wore a red woolly jersey and a little brown cloak. She had rubber shoes on her feet and a woolly hood over her dark curls. She looked the picture of health and happiness, and Hamid, edging up as close as possible, felt very proud of her.

The rain was pouring down one night when the children splashed their way up the cobbles and hammered on the door of their refuge. They shook themselves on the step like wet little dogs, and surged forward towards the fire, puffing and blowing and sniffing. The English nurse felt especially sorry for them, for she thought she had never seen them look so wretched and sad. Yet they lifted their merry, cheeky faces to her and their dark eyes were still bright. She marvelled at their courage.

But there was one well-known little figure missing, and this was the second night he had not turned up – an undersized shrimp of a boy who had come regularly for months.

"Where is Abd-el-Khader?" the nurse asked.

"He can't come," replied one child in a careless voice. "His rags fell right to pieces, and he hasn't a father. He has nothing to wear at all, and he must stay at home till his mother can save enough to buy a sugar-sack."

No one seemed to care or seemed surprised, and the evening passed as usual. But when supper was finished the nurse turned to Hamid, who always lingered to the last. "Do you know where Abd-el-Khader lives?" she asked.

Hamid nodded. "Up at the top of the town by the prickly pear hedges," he replied, "but the path is like a muddy river. You could not go there tonight."

"I think I could," said the nurse, "and if you would like to earn a little money, you can take me there."

Hamid nodded enthusiastically. He liked Abd-el-Khader. He waited at the bottom of the stairs while the nurse went upstairs to sort out some old clothes, and while he waited his bright eyes roamed around the house. He had never been left alone before, and he found it very interesting. He poked his nose into the room on the left and found himself in a little kitchen. On one shelf stood a china bowl of eggs, just low enough for him to help himself.

Hamid hesitated. He could not count, but perhaps the nurse could, and would notice if he took two. On the other hand, raw eggs sucked through a little hole in the top are delicious, and Hamid had not tasted one for a long time. He decided it was worth the risk. If he waited outside the door, the nurse would never see in the darkness. Even if she noticed later, she would not be able to prove it was him.

So he took an egg in each hand, nipped out into the street, and stood waiting in the dark. Soon the nurse appeared with a bundle and a key, and, what Hamid had not bargained for, a powerful torch.

"Come along," said the nurse, turning on her torch. "Walk with me and we can both walk in the light."

But to the nurse's surprise, Hamid did not wish to walk in the light. He seemed to be taking great care to keep out of the the beam, slinking along the gutters, shuffling against the wall. It was very dark and very muddy, and once or twice he slipped, clutching his precious eggs tightly in both hands.

"Why won't you walk with me in the middle of the road?" asked the nurse, puzzled. "You will fall if you run along in the gutter like that."

"I'm all right," muttered Hamid, rather miserably. He was not enjoying himself at all. He was so afraid of that broad beam of light, and the eggs somehow did not seem worth it. He wished he could get rid of them, and yet at the same time he wanted to hold on to them.

It was pitch black away from the torch, and when they started climbing the steep back-alleys Hamid could not see where he was going at all. Suddenly his foot caught on an unexpected step and he fell headlong on his face. He gave a sharp cry of shock and pain, and the nurse, who was a little ahead, turned round quickly and shone the light full on to him.

She saw him struggle to his feet, his gown covered with black mud and yellow egg-yolk. She saw his hands clasping the smashed shells, and his grazed knees streaming with blood, and she understood at once what had happened. He would have scuttled away from her, but she took hold of him quickly, and he burst into frightened tears. He had no idea what she would do. She might fetch the police and put him in prison; or she might beat him in the street. Whatever she did or did not do, he felt sure she would never have him in her house again. Never again would he enter that place of warmth and light. He would be shut out, and it was all his own fault.

Then through his sobs he heard the voice of the nurse speaking quietly to him.

"Come along," she said, "you've cut your knees badly. We'll go home and bandage them up, and then you can show me the way again afterwards." She kept tight hold of him, and they walked home in silence, except for Hamid's sniffs. When they got there, she locked the door on the inside.

Still silent and ashamed, Hamid washed his hands under the tap, and then the nurse sat him down and bathed his black knees till the cuts and grazes were quite clean. She put ointment and bandages on them, then she took a good look at him. He sat slumped in a sorry little heap covered with mud and raw egg. The only clean parts about him were the little tracks on his cheeks made by his tears.

Still without speaking she went upstairs where she kept a bundle of old clothes, and came back with a clean shirt and a grey woolly sweater which had been mended many times. Then she fetched more warm water and soap and scrubbed him clean. Next she dressed him in his new clothes and sat down beside him.

He looked up at her, marvelling, for it was his very first experience of someone returning good for evil, and he could not understand it. Instead of prison and a beating he had been given medicine and clean, beautiful clothes.

"Hamid," said the nurse beside him, "you fell over and hurt yourself because you would not walk in the light with me. You were afraid to walk in the light because you had stolen my eggs."

There was no answer.

"You don't deserve ever to come here again," went on the nurse, "but they were my eggs and I paid for them, so I'm going to forgive you – only you must promise never to steal anything out of my house again."

Hamid nodded.

"And remember," said the nurse, speaking very slowly, "you could not walk in the light with me because of what you had done wrong. Jesus says he is the Light of the world. You must ask him to forgive you for what you did tonight and then you must walk beside him in his light, every day until you get to heaven. He will make you feel clean inside, just like I made you feel clean outside when I washed away the mud and egg."

Hamid looked down at his clean clothes and bandages, and understood. His eggs that had seemed so precious were gone, but he did not want them any more. He had been forgiven and washed and made clean. He had been brought back into the warmth and shelter of the nurse's home. They were going out again into the dark to find Abd-el-Khader's house, but it would be quite different now. He would walk close beside the nurse. He would not stumble, and he would not be afraid of the light any longer, because he no longer had anything to hide. They would walk guided by the torch's bright, steady beam. It would be a treat.

Half an hour later, having finished their task, they returned to the house. The wind roared against the rocks behind the town, and the rain beat up the streets in cold gusts. Hamid said good-bye on the step.

"But where are you going to sleep?" asked the nurse doubtfully.

"In the mosque," answered the little boy.

"But have you any blankets there?"

"No."

"Isn't it very cold?"

"Tonight I shall be warm in my new sweater."

"Well, you can come in tonight and sleep on the floor. The fire is still burning."

So she left him, lying comfortably on the mat, covered with a blanket, staring into the glow of the dying charcoal and thinking over the events of the evening. He had learned something that night that he would never forget all his life. Sitting up suddenly, he held out his hands and whispered the words of a simple hymn he had learned by heart, asking God to give him a clean heart, forgive the bad things he had done, and lead him to heaven.

Chapter Eleven

Christmas

Hamid and Ayashi crept shivering from the mosque one morning to find the olive groves and mountains above the town white with snow. The winter season had come to stay.

One week was particularly cold and bleak, and on a night of drizzling rain the children arrived at the door as usual and knocked impatiently, for the wind seemed to be cutting them in two, and their sodden, fluttering rags clung to their bodies. The door was opened at once, and they tumbled over the threshold, eager to reach the warmth of the fireside. But once inside the passage they stopped suddenly and stared, the cold and the rain forgotten.

For instead of the bright glare of the electric light, they found themselves facing the soft blaze of candles set in a circle on a little table in the middle of the room, with olive branches wreathed around them. On the floor, arranged like a picnic on a coloured cloth, a feast was spread. There were nuts, almonds, raisins, sweets, oranges, bananas, sugar biscuits and honey-cakes, and on a tray in the corner was a shining teapot and a collection of little glasses. A kettle sang merrily on the glowing charcoal, and the room seemed warm and welcoming. Even Kinza had stayed up for the feast. She sat on a cushion, holding a big red and white rubber ball, her face lifted expectantly.

"It's the feast of the Christians today," explained the nurse to the wide-eyed little boys, "so I thought we would keep it together. It is the Feast of the Birth of Jesus Christ. He was the greatest gift God ever gave, so at his Feast we all give presents to each other. That is why Kinza has a rubber ball, and I've bought you all sweets and oranges and bananas."

The children sat down to their feast, shyly at first because of the strangeness of it all; but gradually their tongues loosened, their toes and fingers thawed, and their cheeks flushed. They talked and ate merrily, tucking away their fruit and sweets in their rags to eat later, and sipping glass after glass of hot, sweet mint tea.

Hamid could not take his eyes off Kinza. She was dressed in her very best blue frock and her curls were brushed out like a halo. How round and sturdy she had grown! He suddenly remembered the white-faced, ragged little sister of past winters, the mud in the village, and the poverty and wretchedness. All that seemed shut out now; they seemed to be sitting cut off from the bleak world outside, in a warm, kind circle of candlelight. The children were talking about feasts in general, and he began to talk too. He began telling them about the sheep feast in his own village, and the nurse, watching his eager face, felt glad. He too had changed lately – since the night he took the eggs. He was no longer a shy, fearful little stranger, but took his place confidently every night. She sat watching him, longing to know what had happened in his child-heart, until her attention was suddenly taken by something that was happening beside her.

Kinza had risen to her feet, and there was a look on her face the nurse had never seen before, as if she had remembered something – some dearly-loved sound. Groping forward uncertainly, feeling her way with touch and hearing, she moved towards the speaker and stood beside him, wondering what to do.

At any other time Hamid would have been frightened at his secret being discovered, and would probably have pushed Kinza away. But there was an atmosphere in the room that night that took away fear and suspicion, and Hamid, forgetting everyone else, put his arm round his little sister and drew her to him. She nestled up to him, remembering the voice she loved, and laid her shining head comfortably against his wet rags.

And the nurse, watching in amazement, suddenly noticed how alike they were. Little memories flashed into her mind. The two children had arrived at the same time from nowhere. Hamid had asked to see Kinza asleep, and she had noticed how he secretly watched her in the street. She suddenly felt quite sure that they were brother and sister, but even if she was right, it would make no difference. Hamid was unlikely to tell his secret, and she certainly would not part with Kinza. She could only wonder what sad story had brought them to the city, and be glad that they had been led to her door.

The other children stared too. "She knows his voice," they said wonderingly, and they glanced at each other with surprise. But they could not speak their thoughts in front of the nurse, and soon forgot about it as they drank more glasses of mint tea. Then, when the feast was ended, the nurse asked them to turn round and look at a white sheet hung on the wall. She blew out the flickering candles, and pictures appeared on the sheet. The boys thought it was magic, and watched, wide-eyed and open-mouthed.

It started with a picture of a girl and a man knocking at the door of an inn, but they had to go away because there was no room. Hamid felt sorry for them because he, too, on his first night in town, had stood and gazed into the inn, longing for shelter. He had had no money, so he had slept on the rubbish heap, but the couple had gone into the stable and the next picture showed them inside with the cattle. But a wonderful thing had happened. She had given birth to a baby son, and wrapped him in cloth and laid him in the manger. Hamid remembered how his mother had wrapped up Kinza, and she had slept in a wooden cradle. This baby was the child of very poor people, no doubt.

But what was the nurse saying? The baby in the

manger was Jesus Christ, whose birth all Christians celebrated. He was God's great gift, and he had come willingly. The stable in the picture looked rather dark, lit only by one small lantern, but the home of the Son of God in heaven was bright with the light of glory and love. Why had he left it?

The nurse was just telling them, "though he was rich, yet for your sakes he became poor. He left the light and came into the dark, a homeless child, so he could lead people to the shelter and love of his father, God."

And now there was a third picture. There were shepherds on the hillside, keeping watch over their flocks by night. Hamid thought of his own goats, and the days he had spent with them on the mountain. Another picture appeared, of an angel appearing to the shepherds, who were afraid. "Fear not – unto you is born a Saviour," said the angel. The sheep grazed on contentedly – there was peace in heaven and goodwill on earth.

Then the last picture was flashed on the screen. The shepherds were kneeling, barefoot, in their rough fleece coats, worshipping the king of heaven who had become a homeless child, lying in a manger amongst the cattle.

It was over. The nurse switched on the lights, and the pictures faded. There was nothing left of the feast except the burnt-out candles, sweet papers, orange peel and banana skins. But the thought of a love that gave, and of a love that became poor, stayed with Hamid as he stepped thoughtfully out into the wet street. Kinza stood in the doorway, waving as they went, and as he passed he put out a shy hand and touched her hair.

The other boys had gone on ahead, but Hamid loitered along slowly, the pictures still bright in his head, not noticing the drizzling rain.

As he passed under a street-lamp, a sharp little mewing caught his ears, and looking down he saw a skeleton-like kitten, very small and wet, trying to shelter behind a drain-pipe.

In his eleven years of life he had seen many starving kittens dying in the street, and had never given them two seconds' thought. But tonight it was somehow different. He could not possibly have explained, but the first seeds of gentleness had been sown in his heart. He found to his surprise that he cared about the starving little creature, and he picked it up and held it against him. It was so thin that its skin seemed to be stretched tightly over its bones, and he could feel its heart beating rapidly.

What should he do with it? He had no doubts at all. There was one open door where it would certainly be welcome, and Kinza would probably love it. It would be his Christmas gift to her.

He pattered back over the cobbles and knocked at the nurse's door. When she opened it, he held out the shivering, wretched creature with perfect confidence.

"It's for Kinza," he explained, "a gift of the feast. It is very hungry and cold, so I brought it to you."

The nurse hesitated. The last thing she really wanted just then was a half-dead ginger kitten, covered with sores and fleas, but she could not refuse, because she knew why he had given it. With a thrill of joy she realised that her evening's work had not been in vain. One little boy at least understood, and entered into the spirit of Christmas. He had wanted to give, and he had been gentle and kind to an outcast kitten. It was the first time she had ever seen a local child care about the sufferings of an animal.

So she accepted it gratefully and joyfully, and then holding it at arm's length she carried it to a box near the fire and sprinkled it all over with disinfectant powder. Then she gave it a saucer of milk, and it twitched its tail at a cheeky angle and lapped it up – a tough, brave little kitten that deserved to be saved!

As she sat watching it, a funny picture came into her mind which left her laughing. She imagined all the Christmas love-gifts before the manger – the gold, frankincense and myrrh – and perched on top of the glittering pile, precious in the eyes of the one to whom it was given, was a thin, flea-ridden, ginger kitten, with its tail sticking up in the air – the sign of a little boy's love and care.

Chapter Twelve

Jenny

Many, many miles away there was a different Christmas party taking place. The children here were also feeling very happy and carefree, like the ones in the nurse's home.

But it was a quite different kind of party. Instead of oranges and nuts and sweets there were jellies and trifles and chocolate biscuits, and a big Christmas cake, and instead of black, wet rags there were brightly-coloured dresses and sweaters, and the girls had bright ribbons in their hair. It should have been a perfect party, and yet when the tea and games were over, and the joyful children gathered by the Christmas tree to sing carols, the grown-up visitors all felt sad, and one small visitor, aged nine, felt saddest of all.

For this was a Blind School, and the little singers

with their bright faces could not see the tree or the candles or the toys they had been given. They had eaten their meal excitedly, and danced merrily up and down to the sound of music, and now they were singing with all their hearts. Jenny, sitting in the audience with her parents, felt very sad. If she always had to live in the dark she was quite certain she would never be happy again. She shut her eyes for a moment, and tried to imagine what it would be like to be blind, but it was really too dreadful even to think about, so she opened them again quickly and watched the children.

They were singing a carol that Jenny herself had learned at school:

Star of wonder, star of light,
Star with royal beauty bright,
Westward leading, still proceeding,
Guide us to thy perfect Light.

Jenny wondered why they had been taught such words. What was the good of singing about perfect light when they were doomed to spend all their days in darkness? Yet, as she watched them, she had to admit to herself that not one little singer looked unhappy.

Jenny knew the story of that carol, for they had made a beautiful wall picture of it to decorate the classroom for their Christmas party. Their teacher had stuck on the brightly coloured figures – three lurching camels, three wise men with long white beards and their treasures of gold, frankincense and myrrh; a shining star beaming down on a humble little house where a poor woman sat playing with her baby boy.

Jenny's mother touched her and she stopped dreaming and started clapping very loudly so that the blind children should hear how pleased she was. And then it was over, and the children crowded round to say goodbye, touching and feeling and chattering, and the smallest ones were carried away happy and sleepy to bed. But the bigger ones stayed round the doorway to wave and shout to the sound of cars driving away, and that was the last Jenny saw of them.

She was very quiet on the way home, and her mother, thinking she was tired, hurried her up to her room, lit her gas fire and bustled her into bed. For Jenny had been ill, and this had been her first real outing for three months. Her mother had wondered whether she ought to go, but Jenny had insisted, and as usual had got her way. Her father had recently joined the council of the Blind School and they had all been invited to the Christmas party.

Jenny nestled down under her pink duvet and looked at all her Christmas presents – the books, the games, the cosy new dressing-gown, the little gold wrist-watch and the travelling case. It had been a good Christmas, and the best present of all – a pony of her own – was down in the stable. For the first time in her rather self-centred life Jenny suddenly realised that she was really a very fortunate child. She thought of the blind children with the toys they could not see, and the children out in Morocco who had no toys at all, and often no food. Her Aunt Rosemary looked after some of them, and had written her an early Christmas letter all about them, and Jenny had been thrilled. It had been like a new, exciting story, giving her a peep into a world she knew nothing about, a world where children like herself went about in rags, and earned their own living, and slept by themselves out of doors – a world where little babies got ill because they didn't have enough to eat. Jenny adored babies, but the only ones she had ever met had nannies who took care of them, and she had not been allowed to hold them in her arms as she had longed to do. These other babies were probably too poor to have nannies, and perhaps she would be allowed to pick them up.

For the wonderful thing was that in a very short time Jenny would actually see the children that Aunt Rosemary had written about. Only six weeks after Christmas, she and her parents were going by car on a long journey to visit her and her beggar-children in the mountains of North Africa.

The doctor had said that Jenny needed sunshine. She had had plenty of medicines, creams, tonics and drives out in the car, but you cannot get warm sunshine in England in January, so they were going southwards to a land of blue skies and yellow beaches and calm seas, where she would grow strong and brown and healthy.

She sleepily wondered how her father would know the way, and supposed they would just follow the sun, as the Wise Men had followed the star. When her mother returned with a drink and biscuits on a tray she found her little daughter fast asleep. She stood looking down on the flushed face and tumbled hair for a moment, then put out the light, opened the big window, and slipped away, leaving Jenny to dream of stars, sunshine and Christmas trees.

Chapter Thirteen

The holiday begins

Very early one morning in March, the English
nurse woke, got out of bed at once, and ran up to
her flat roof to look at the weather. It was going to
be a fine day, she decided happily, and this was
just as it should be, for this was the day she had
looked forward to for so long. Her cousin from
England was arriving to stay in the hotel for a fortnight. Her husband was coming with her, and they
were bringing Jenny.

It was the thought of Jenny that made the English
nurse very happy. She woke Kinza, who was lying
in a ball on a mattress on the floor, her ginger
kitten close beside her. The first thing she always
did on waking was to stretch out her hand and
make sure that the kitten was there, and if it had
gone for a walk she made a terrible fuss. But this
morning all was well.

Hand in hand the English nurse and Kinza climbed the stairs on to the flat roof, and sat down at a low round table, eating breakfast together under a blue spring sky.

"The little girl is coming today," announced the nurse, as she tidied up and tried not to trip over Kinza and the kitten, who were playing on the floor with a ball. "We are going to take a holiday. We will go to the market together and buy nice things to eat, and then we'll make a feast for the little girl."

"A feast! A feast!" shouted Kinza, jumping about like a clumsy goat kid, and falling over the waste-paper basket. "I will carry the basket for you. Let's go now."

"Yes, let's," said the nurse, and off they went into the sunshine hand in hand. She had not had a weekday holiday for a long time. She usually stayed inside in the morning. But today she had told the people not to come. She was going to be free to get ready for Jenny, and now, while it was still early, she was going to climb up the hillside behind the town and pick flowers.

It was too far for Kinza, so when they had done their shopping she left her on the step of the doughnut shop in the charge of Hamid. She often did this when she was busy, for she felt quite sure that the two children were probably brother and sister and should spend some time together. Kinza was always perfectly safe and happy when Hamid looked after her, although she sometimes ended up rather greasy, and not very keen on her dinner. She was very fond of doughnuts, and would eat all that were offered her.

Once by herself, the nurse almost ran up the steep, cobbled streets, past the tumbledown shacks on the outskirts of the town and out through the gate in the ruined wall that led on to the hillside. She suddenly forgot that she would soon be middle-aged and felt very young indeed. She began picking the flowers which were growing all around her.

"How beautiful they are!" she thought. "I shall bring Jenny up here and we'll pick them together."

As she thought of Jenny, she began to wonder how they would all get on together. Their lives were so different. Once, when they had been growing up together, she and Elizabeth had been like sisters, but Elizabeth had married a rich man and had gone to live in his beautiful home. Jenny had been brought up surrounded by beauty and peace, and had had everything that love and money could give. Aunt Rosemary could have made her home with them too, but while she was training to be a nurse she had felt that God wanted her to go to Africa to help people and to care for poor, ragged children. Elizabeth and her husband thought it was a foolish thing to do and Aunt Rosemary had found it difficult to write and tell them about her life.

Their letters had mainly been about Jenny, and every Christmas Elizabeth had sent Rosemary a photograph of her as she grew up and she had kept them all in a little photo-album. The last picture had been of Jenny on her pony. Rosemary wondered how Jenny would feel about the simple toys the Moorish children enjoyed. She was used to expensive dolls and proper cots, and riding her pony about her father's estate. She would probably get very bored. Feeling rather sad, Rosemary hurried back down the mountain with her flowers, collected a happy, sticky Kinza, and went home.

She went to the toy cupboard and inspected it rather sadly.There were some shabby scrap-books, faded puzzles and chipped bricks, some scruffy little dolls and a box of stubby chalks. They had all obviously been enjoyed by children who had never seen toys before, and were well worn. Aunt Rosemary shut the cupboard with a sigh, and went to the kitchen to make buns.

By half-past four the little house was as bright as scrubbing and polishing could make it, and the sitting room was sweet with the scent of wild flowers. Tea was ready, the kettle was singing on the stove, and Aunt Rosemary and Kinza set out to meet the car in front of the hotel.

It arrived punctually, a smart, streamlined vehicle, and the little boys surged round, fighting each other in their efforts to carry the luggage. Aunt Rosemary stood waiting for them to get out, and above the pandemonium she heard a child's voice cry out, "Oh, Mummy, look! What a sweet little girl! You never told me Aunt Rosemary had a little girl."

And then the next moment they had extricated themselves from the mob of little boys, and Elizabeth, looking just as young as she had looked ten years before, was kissing her cousin warmly. Jenny was squatting on the ground, trying to make friends with Kinza.

"Jenny," said her mother sharply, "you haven't greeted Aunt Rosemary."

Jenny got up, kissed her aunt politely and turned back to Kinza. While the adults sorted out the luggage, passports and forms, Aunt Rosemary stood quietly watching the child whom for years she had longed to see. An elfin-looking child, she thought to herself, and went over to make friends.

Jenny turned a troubled face to her aunt.

"What is the matter with this little girl?" she asked wonderingly. "I showed her my pretty brooch, and she just stared in front of her."

"I'm afraid she's blind, Jenny," said Aunt Rosemary gently. "But it doesn't mean you can't play with her. You must give her toys she can feel, and you must sing to her, and let her touch you. She'll soon love you."

She lifted Kinza's tiny hand and passed it lightly over Jenny's face and hair. "That's how she gets to know people," she explained, and then turned to speak to Jenny's mother and father. But before she could say anything Jenny had seized her mother's hand and was looking up at her, her grey eyes brimming with tears.

"She's blind, Mummy," she whispered, "like the little Christmas children."

"Never mind," replied Mrs Swift gently. "She looks a very happy little girl, and we must find her a little present. Now let's come and see Aunt Rosemary's house."

They set off across the market, the grown-ups walking ahead, and Jenny leading Kinza, too interested in her new playmate to notice much of the town about her. She was happier than she had been all the holiday, for, much as she loved her mother and father, she was only nine, and she longed for other children to play with. Most of all she longed for something to look after. She was too old for dolls, her pets had all been left at home, and she missed them dreadfully. But a curly-haired blind baby of three was far better than pets. She had never dreamed of anything so exciting.

They had reached the narrow back street where Aunt Rosemary lived, and Mrs Swift was talking in rather a strained voice and trying not to look too horrified at the babies sitting on the cobbles, and the ragged old beggar chanting in one of the door-ways. Then she suddenly looked very horrified indeed, for Aunt Rosemary had stopped in front of the last house, and was taking out her key. On the doorstep sat a very poor woman, holding some-thing to her breast, under her rags.

Rosemary spoke to the woman, who pulled aside her rags and held out a baby, all skin and bones, half-dead with sickness and exhaustion. Mrs Swift put out her hand to take hold of Jenny, but she was too late. Her child had stepped forward, and both she and Aunt Rosemary were stooping over the pathetic little creature, quite absorbed.

"Jenny!" commanded her mother. "Come here!" But Jenny took not the slightest notice. She turned tragic eyes to her aunt.

"Is it going to die?" she whispered.

"I don't know; I hope not," replied Aunt Rosemary. "Let's come in."

She opened the front door, led the woman into the room where she gave out the medicines, and told her to sit down while she turned back to her guests. Mrs Swift was standing very still, recovering from her shock at finding such a wretched creature on Rosemary's doorstep. She noticed that the young mother had a patient face, one used to suffering, with beautiful dark eyes that gleamed with hope as she lifted her baby towards the nurse.

"Rosemary," she urged, "don't worry about us; we can look after ourselves. You go and see to that poor baby."

Aunt Rosemary hesitated.

"Well, come upstairs," she said, "and I can show you where the sitting-room is. Tea is all ready, and the kettle is boiling."

It was a surprise to enter a house in that dingy street and find it bright with pictures and flowers, and a delicious meal set out on pretty china. Aunt Rosemary sat them down on the low mattress seats and made tea. Then she spoke rather shyly.

"It seems awfully rude," she said, "but would you mind if I left you just for ten minutes? You see, I know this woman. She's lost four babies – this one is all she's got."

Jenny slipped her hand into her aunt's.

"I'm coming to help you," she announced.

"No, Jenny," exclaimed her mother firmly, "it's quite out of the question. Come and sit down and eat your tea."

Jenny flew into a passion at once.

"I want to go!" she stormed. "I want to see that baby get well. I don't want any tea! Say I can come, Aunt Rosemary – it's your house. Daddy, say I can go. Mummy, you might let me..."

Her father most unexpectedly came to Jenny's rescue.

"What is the matter with that baby?" he asked.

"Has it got anything infectious?"

"I shouldn't think so," answered Aunt Rosemary. "I've seen it before. It's suffering from starvation and wrong feeding."

"Then, Elizabeth, I should let her go, if Rosemary doesn't mind," said Mr Swift. As Jenny left the room triumphantly, he turned to his wife.

"Darling," he said, "let her help all she can. She needs to help someone. It may make her a little less selfish to see that sort of thing, and I'm sure Rosemary will be sensible about infection."

"Perhaps so," agreed Jenny's mother, and she gave a little sigh. "If only she could have had younger brothers and sisters," she added wistfully.

Meanwhile Jenny and her aunt were bending over the white-faced baby, and the mother was telling the usual tale of poverty, ignorance and wrong feeding. It seemed almost too late to help, but perhaps there was still a chance. Aunt Rosemary, nursing the tiny thing in a blanket, turned to Jenny.

"Go upstairs, Jenny," she said, "and bring me a cup and a spoon and some sugar from the shelf above the stove."

Jenny obeyed, moving swiftly and lightly.

"And now go and fetch the kettle," commanded her aunt.

Jenny was off in a flash.

"Now bring me those white tablets on the third shelf over there," went on her aunt, speaking very gravely, and Jenny had the uncomfortable feeling that her aunt disapproved of her.

"Now, please, rinse out the cup and spoon with some of that boiled water... now crush up one tablet... mix it with a very little water... pass me that bottle..."

Jenny forgot her temper, forgot her aunt, and forgot herself. She knelt perfectly still on the mat, only conscious of the weak gurgling sound as the baby tried to swallow. Almost drop by drop the medicine disappeared and the baby was not sick. It took a few more spoonfuls of sweetened water, and then Aunt Rosemary began talking to the mother in Arabic, explaining that she must sit quietly for an hour and then they would give the child another drink.

"It must get better," muttered Jenny to herself. "It must! It must!"

And then Aunt Rosemary did something that surprised Jenny. She pointed to the picture on the wall, of Jesus holding a child in his arms, and told the woman all about it, and then she prayed aloud for the little sick baby. Jenny could not understand what her aunt was saying, but she knew she was praying.

I wonder if that really does any good, thought Jenny to herself, and she too glanced up at the painting on the wall, and somehow the sight of the child in the picture being held so closely made the real baby seem safer.

"It's sure to get better," breathed Jenny to herself, bending over it again. And as she watched, the weak eyelids fluttered, and the baby opened its eyes.

Chapter Fourteen

A light begins to shine

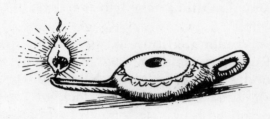

They didn't need to make any further plans, for Jenny announced firmly that they were going to stay in the town until it was time to go home to England, and she was going to be Kinza's nurse and help Aunt Rosemary every day with the sick babies in the clinic.

Mr Swift laughed comfortably, and then wondered what he was going to do with himself in a remote mountain village for two weeks. Mrs Swift sighed anxiously and insisted that Jenny should gargle three times a day. Jenny herself was openly thrilled and Aunt Rosemary was secretly very happy. She felt the holiday was going to be a complete success.

It was Sunday afternoon, and on Sunday no one came to the clinic. There had been a meeting for women in the afternoon, and Jenny watched them leaving, walking slowly down the street with their babies tied tightly on their backs, under the white outer garments that covered them from head to toe.

"They look like camels with humps, carrying their babies like that," remarked Jenny. "You'd think their babies would be suffocated, wouldn't you? Why don't they have baby carriers, like ordinary people?"

"They couldn't afford to buy them," replied Aunt Rosemary, smiling, "but it certainly isn't a very good way to carry them. A lot of babies grow up with weak chests through lack of fresh air. You've noticed how pale some of them look."

"And spotty, and thin and dirty," added Jenny, wrinkling her small nose. "It's a pity there aren't more people like you to teach them how to look after their babies properly. You know, Auntie, I've been thinking, and I've decided that when I grow up I'm going to be a missionary, too, and I'm going to come out here, and have a clinic and make all the sick people better like you do. I think it's such fun."

Aunt Rosemary looked down into Jenny's brown, confident face, and she didn't answer for a moment or two.

"You couldn't be a missionary unless something very important happened to you first, Jenny," she said at last.

"Why not, Auntie?" enquired Jenny, surprised. "I could learn to be a nurse and how to look after babies. I wouldn't need to know anything else, would I?"

"Yes, I think you would," replied Aunt Rosemary with a smile, "but I'm not going to tell you just here in the passage. Let's take a picnic tea to the Tower Gardens, and then we can talk about it. Kinza will be awake by now, and she loves the Tower Gardens."

"Ooh, lovely!" cried Jenny, and pranced up the stairs two at a time to get things ready. "Mummy said I could stay to tea if you invited me. I specially asked her."

"Did you, now?" said Aunt Rosemary, laughing. "Would you like to get Kinza ready while I get the picnic? Then we can go."

Ten minutes later Aunt Rosemary, Jenny and Kinza were climbing the steps to the Tower Gardens, which were so beautiful they stood still for a moment, gazing at everything silently.

"Don't let Kinza fall in the pond," warned Aunt Rosemary. "You just hang on to her while I spread out the tea."

She unpacked the basket and then sat for a few moments quietly watching the two children at play. Kinza was growing into a beautiful little girl now, strong and sturdy. Who was she, and what would become of her? It was time some practical plan was made about her future, thought Aunt Rosemary to herself, if she was to grow up useful and clever with her hands. And Jenny – was she going to grow up careless and selfish? She hoped not.

Jenny caught sight of the picnic laid out, and, taking Kinza's hand in hers, came running up. Kinza was given a bun, and Jenny helped herself to a sandwich and turned her questioning face to her aunt.

"What else would I have to know to become a missionary?" she asked, as though the conversation had never left off.

"It depends on what you want to do," replied Aunt Rosemary steadily. "If you simply want to heal people's sickness, then you must train to be a nurse or a doctor. But most of them are so poor that they will probably get ill again very quickly, and in any case none of our bodies last very long. The part of people that really matters is the part that lasts for ever, their real proper selves, which we call their spirits. You can only really help them and make them happy by leading them to the Lord Jesus, and you can't possibly do that unless you know him yourself. So it isn't really *what* you know, but *who* you know."

"But you spend such a long time each day giving them medicine," said Jenny. "Why couldn't I just do that?"

"You could," said Aunt Rosemary, "but the reason I do it is not just to make them better. I give it because I want them to see that Jesus lives in me and he cares about their pain, and wants to help them. You have got to *show* the love of Jesus by doing good things. He isn't on earth any more, but his spirit lives in the hearts of those who love and trust him, and he works through them. So the first thing you have to be sure of is that Jesus is actually there, loving through you. Otherwise it's just like taking an empty lantern out in the dark."

"Well, how do you know if he's there or not?" asked Jenny.

"How does the light get into the empty lantern?" asked Aunt Rosemary. "It's just a matter of opening a door and placing a candle inside. Jesus is the light, and he wants to come in. If the glass of the lantern is clean, the light shines out clearly, but if the glass is cloudy and dirty the light will be very dim. If we really want him to, Jesus will make us clean and new inside, like clear glass, by helping us to stop being bad-tempered and impatient and disobedient. Then the light of Jesus's love will shine through, and people will be attracted to him. He is the important part, not the lantern."

There was another pause.

"So I suppose only very good people can be missionaries?" Jenny said thoughtfully.

"It's not exactly that," said Aunt Rosemary. "Many people are very good and kind without Jesus, just like golden lanterns when you put them in the sun. But in the evening the sun sets. Our own goodness lasts only as long as we do – until we die. The love and life and goodness of Jesus last for ever, and the person who has his light in them will last for ever as well. It is what is called eternal life, and of course it's a far stronger sort of goodness than the other kind."

"There are Mummy and Daddy coming into the garden," exclaimed Jenny suddenly, and she jumped up and ran along the path towards them. She was rather glad to escape from this conversation, for Aunt Rosemary was saying some quite disturbing things, and Jenny did not really like being disturbed. But whatever happened, she knew she would always be by far the most important person in the world to her mother and father.

Aunt Rosemary followed, leading a rather crumby Kinza. She smiled at Elizabeth over Jenny's head – it was wonderful to see her running about and strong again. One of the best parts of the holiday for both women had been the renewing of their old friendship, which now felt as strong and sure as it had done before their very different ways of life had seemed to separate them. Elizabeth had to admit that her cousin was not altogether wasting her time. The look on the face of the sick baby's mother had taught her that, and in spite of the germs and the sores at the clinic, she trusted Rosemary with Jenny as she had never trusted anyone before. And this was strange, for a few weeks ago she would have been horrified at her little girl having anything to do with poverty and illness.

There are different sorts of beauty, she had thought to herself. Healing and helping and loving and giving are beautiful. I want Jenny to grow up good and unselfish, and I think Rosemary can help her in that way.

When she spoke to her husband about it, he agreed. "She's learning something practical in that clinic," he said, "and she may find she'd make a good nurse."

"Rosemary," said Elizabeth, cuddling Kinza against her, "couldn't you desert your little ones just for once this evening, and come and have supper with us at the hotel?"

"They don't come on Sunday," replied Rosemary. "It's my day off, except for the afternoon meeting. I'd love to come."

"Oh, Mummy, look!" cried Jenny. "That peacock has spread open his tail." And she hurried her parents off to see, while Rosemary and Kinza made their slow way home.

An hour later Rosemary was sitting in the big hotel dining room, under a cut-glass chandelier, eating a four-course dinner with Jenny and her parents, who had all dressed up in their very best to welcome her. It was a great treat to Rosemary to come out to supper, and there was always so much to say when she and Elizabeth got together. Tonight the conversation turned to Kinza.

"She's such a beautiful little creature," said Elizabeth, "it seems so cruel she should be blind. What are you going to do with her in the future, Rosemary?"

"I would like her to go to some training school in about three years' time," said Rosemary, "where she can learn Braille and basket-work. She could earn her own living like that out here, and when she was really good she could come back to me."

Jenny leaned forward across the table, nearly upsetting her glass in her eagerness.

"The Blind School, Daddy!" she cried, "where they invited us all at Christmas. If Kinza went there, Mummy, she could come and stay with us sometimes, and I'd look after her. It would be like having a little sister, and I'd see her lots and lots, and she'd be so happy if I was there. They had such a lovely time at Christmas. Oh, when can she come, Auntie Rosemary? Couldn't we take her home with us this time?"

The cousins looked at each other questioningly.

"It's not a bad idea of Jenny's," said Mrs Swift. "It's a very good school, and they take them quite young. John could easily get her in free. He's on the board and has a lot of influence. The sooner she goes, the more quickly she'd learn English.

Also, she could travel with us in the car instead of you having to bring her."

Rosemary hesitated. She just didn't know what to answer. It was all so sudden. Jenny was jumping up and down in her chair in her excitement.

"Jenny gets tired of these long car drives," added Mrs Swift. "She's always so much happier if there's another child in the car."

"I just don't know what to say," replied Rosemary. "It's really very kind of you... but somehow she seems so small to go away just yet. Could I think it over and give you an answer in a day or two?"

"Of course," answered Mrs Swift. "Just let us know when you feel sure. No, Jenny, don't go on and on about it. People can't make up their minds on important matters without a little 'think' first, or they may make them up wrongly."

"I've made mine up on this important matter," announced Jenny dramatically. "Oh, Auntie Rosemary, I'm sure you'll say yes. It really does seem to be the best idea I've had in my whole life. Even Mummy and Daddy think it's good. Oh, look, Daddy, there are ice-creams for pudding, the kind you don't like. Please will you pretend you'd like one, and I'll eat it for you as well as mine."

In her excitement at the possibility of getting two ice-creams, Jenny forgot about Kinza for the moment and they talked about other things until Rosemary got up to go.

"John and I will take you home," said Mrs Swift, getting up. "Jenny, darling, run up to bed."

"All right," answered Jenny, who, having enjoyed two ice-creams, was in a good mood.

She flung her arms round her aunt's neck and pulled her head down close to her mouth, so that no one could hear what they were saying.

"You are going to think hard about it, aren't you, Auntie?" she whispered.

"Yes, Jenny, very hard. I'm going to ask God to show me the right way, too."

"Do you think he'll have shown you by tomorrow morning?"

"I don't know, Jenny – it's such a big thing. Give me two days!"

"Well, ask him to show you as quickly as possible – and ask him to let it be Yes."

"Couldn't you ask too?"

"I don't really know how to... but I'll try. Goodnight, Auntie Rosemary."

"Goodnight, Jenny."

She gently loosened the child's clinging arms, and set out across the dark market-place with Mr and Mrs Swift. Under the street lamp she turned to wave, and Jenny waved back, black against the bright background of the huge doorway.

Chapter Fifteen

Jenny learns a hard lesson

Hamid welcomed the coming of spring and the warmer weather. Winter is hard when your only clothes are rags – the clothes that the English nurse had given him had fallen to pieces, but this no longer mattered. Now the sun shone warm and comforting, the storks nested in the towers, flowers clothed the mountain, and cherry and peach blossom made the valley beautiful. Baby goats skipped and jostled in the streets, and Hamid, like all other young things, had grown several inches and looked more like a scarecrow than ever. He sat now on the step of the doughnut stall, licking the oil off his fingers and watching the seething market with bright, observant eyes.

There was always so much to see on market days and amidst all the busyness of people coming and going, Hamid saw Kinza in a scarlet jersey prancing along between Jenny and the English nurse who had come out to do her shopping.

Then in a flash he caught sight of something else. He thought he was dreaming for a second, and rubbed his eyes and looked again. He was not dreaming. He went white under his tan, turned a backward somersault into the shop and hid himself securely between the stone oven and the doughnut counter. Then he peeped out, like a startled rabbit from its hole, to watch what would happen next.

His step-father stood rigid in a doorway opposite, staring fixedly at the little group who were buying oranges, unaware of him. Then, drawing a step or two nearer, he watched Kinza as a snake might watch a baby rabbit at play, waiting its moment to strike. His keen eyes were taking in everything – the blind gestures, the happy freedom of her baby talk, the stout little shoes and the warm clothes. As the three went over to the oil-merchant's he followed, coming so close to his step-daughter that for one breathless moment Hamid wondered if he was going to snatch her up. But he did not touch her. He merely moved behind them, unnoticed in the jostling crowd, and Hamid saw that his black eyes burned with anger and his mouth was closed as tightly as a steel trap.

Hamid, recovering from his first shock, was not afraid. His step-father had come to the market on business and would probably leave the town that evening. He had not seen Hamid, nor would he see him, for at the earliest possible moment Hamid would run off into the mountains and keep company with the monkeys until after dark. He did not worry about Kinza at all – she was in the safe keeping of the English nurse, who loved her and would never let her go. Her home was a fortress which Si Mohamed could never enter.

Hamid's master arrived quite soon, and was surprised and annoyed to find his assistant under the counter instead of behind it. He boxed his ears, which Hamid did not mind in the least, and took some money off his pay, which he minded quite a lot. Once released, his nimble brown feet crisscrossed the danger-zone of the market-place, where his step-father lurked, and he made for the cobbled path that ran along the outskirts of the town.

Kinza, Jenny and Aunt Rosemary made their way home, and never noticed the sinister figure of the man who followed them as far as the entrance of the street and stood watching until the door of the house closed behind them. It was almost time for the clinic to open. Usually, while Aunt Rosemary worked there, Kinza sat on the front step in the sunshine and talked to her kitten, and the patients stepped over or round her. But during the past fortnight she had often been to play with Jenny, who loved looking after her. So now, with her new story book which she had brought to show her aunt in one hand, and Kinza holding on to the other, Jenny set off to find her mother and father at the hotel.

The little girls threaded their way through the market crowds and entered the Tower Gardens which lay between them and the hotel. There was no one in the gardens, for everyone was busy in the market, and the sleepy silence made Jenny want to linger. She thought of her new book; she had just reached an exciting part, and this would be a lovely quiet place to sit and read just for five minutes. Her mother had told her she was never to stop between her aunt's house and the hotel, but after all, her mother did not know what time she set out. She sat down in a pleasant little stone corner near the old archway, with Kinza beside her, and began to read her book.

It was a story about a child just like Jenny, who had a pony of her own and rode in gymkhanas, just as she was going to do when she got home. She hardly noticed that Kinza had got up and started to wander along the path towards the archway. Kinza often went for little walks, her arms held out in front of her to avoid danger. When she felt she had gone far enough she would stand still and squeak till someone fetched her back.

Jenny read on eagerly, for she wanted to reach the end of the chapter and discover whether Annabel's pony was going to win the cup for jumping or not. Out of the corner of her eye she could see Kinza standing in the archway. She must fetch her back in a minute.

She skimmed to the end and got up quickly with a sigh of relief, because Annabel had won easily. But she felt guilty for having let Kinza stray through the archway alone. "Kinza!" she called eagerly, running into the other part of the gardens, and then she stopped short and her eyes grew big with fright.

For the green grass in front of her was empty and deserted – there was no sign of Kinza anywhere.

With her heart beating wildly she ran from bush to bush, searching behind every one; up and down the steps she flew, back into the walled garden, but it was no good. Kinza had completely disappeared.

Jenny rushed out into the market, half-blind with panic, bumping into people who turned to look at her anxiously, pushing her way in and out, searching frantically, with her pale tear-stained cheeks and big, frightened eyes.

At last she stood still, completely out of breath, and because there was nowhere else to look, and because she did not like the people staring at her, she went back to the garden and stood alone by the archway, trying to decide what to do next.

She simply could not go back. Aunt Rosemary had trusted her alone with Kinza, and she had failed completely in her trust. What would her aunt say? And, worse still, where was Kinza? Had something terrible happened to her? Was she frightened or hurt and crying out, wondering why Jenny did not come to her? Jenny did not know. She burst into tears and ran sobbing to the hotel, up the stairs to her mother's room, and into her arms.

When Mrs Swift finally managed to understand what had happened she went rather white, too. She dried Jenny's eyes and took her by the hand.

"We must go and tell Auntie Rosemary at once," she said quietly. "We'll have one more look in the market-place on the way."

Jenny stood quite still. "I *can't* go to Aunt Rosemary," she said tragically, "I just *can't*, Mummy. You'll have to go and tell her."

"No," said Mrs Swift, still quietly, but very firmly, "you must come and tell her yourself. You see, Jenny, this has happened because you were disobedient and untrustworthy, and you must be brave

110

and take the blame you deserve. And we must go now, at once, because if anyone has taken Kinza, every moment may matter. Daddy will come with us."

It was a silent little party that set out from the hotel. Mr Swift suggested that he should do one more quick search of the market-place while Jenny and her mother searched the gardens again. Ten minutes later they met again, solemn and worried.

"Well," said Mr Swift, "the sooner we get Rosemary on to this the better. She can speak the language and question people."

They met Rosemary coming across the market to look for Kinza at the hotel, as it was dinner time. Mr Swift told her what had happened, and while he spoke, Jenny stood a little apart, her eyes fixed on the ground, not daring to look at her aunt's face. She wondered what she would say, and whether she would be angry with her right there in the middle of the market. But nothing was said about her carelessness just then. Everyone seemed to have forgotten about it. All they were thinking about was Kinza.

They went back to the walled garden, to see the exact place so that Aunt Rosemary could question the shop-keepers nearest the spot, but no one could give her any news. Whatever had happened had happened just the other side of the archway, and the archway was hidden from the road by a high wall. There were three exits from that part of the garden, and one led straight out on to a lonely country road that branched off in the next couple of miles into a dozen wild mountain tracks.

"There are two possibilities," said Aunt

Rosemary at last, when all questioning had proved useless. "One is that she has been kidnapped for the sake of her clothes, and in that case the police might help us; the other is that her own people have decided they want her back again and have stolen her away. In that case I'm afraid she has gone for good. After all, I have no claim against her own people. I don't even know where she came from in the first place; I only know she was not a local child." She stopped short as a new idea came into her head. "I wonder where Hamid is," she went on eagerly, "I've often thought he had something to do with her – he might be able to give us some clue."

But not one of the boys who had collected to see what was going on knew where Hamid was. He had been at his job that morning, and had last been seen heading for the mountains. Everyone volunteered to go and look for him, and they scattered in all directions, for the Englishman would no doubt reward the finder handsomely. But no one succeeded in finding him, for he was far up the ravine between the great rocks, throwing stones at the monkeys. So frightened was he of meeting his step-father that he stayed there till long after sunset and missed the boys' meeting for the first time in many weeks.

The police, when they had heard the story, were polite and sympathetic, but not very hopeful. They promised to phone the Government outposts in the mountains to watch the main tracks and check up on travellers. But even if the child was found, what was there to prove that she did not belong to her captors?

There was no more they could do, so they went sorrowfully back to Aunt Rosemary's house to have some tea, but none of them felt hungry, and after a while Mr and Mrs Swift got up to go, and Jenny, pale and wretched, followed them, still not daring to look at her aunt, who had actually hardly given her naughtiness a thought yet. She was far too worried thinking what could have happened to Kinza.

Rosemary was glad to be left alone. She carried out the tea things and then came back into her little room and knelt down, meaning to pray for Kinza. But the kitten sprang up beside her, mewing for its little playmate, and under the cushion on which she rested her arms was something hard and knobbly – Kinza's wooden doll. She gazed round the room, and there was Kinza's ball, Kinza's mat, Kinza's box of sweets that Jenny had given her. Everywhere she looked there were signs of the missing, loved little girl, and Rosemary suddenly laid down her head on her arms and cried. Where was Kinza? What was happening to her? How terrified and homesick she would be, how helpless in her blind darkness! "Oh God," she cried, "take care of her; don't let her be hurt or afraid; bring her back safely to me."

As she prayed she heard a little sob behind her and realised she was not alone in the room. She looked up quickly, and there in the doorway stood Jenny, white-faced and swollen-eyed with crying.

"Jenny!" exclaimed Rosemary, surprised. "Does Mummy know you've come?"

"Yes," said Jenny with a gulp. "I said I must see you alone, so Mummy brought me back to the door, and you'd forgotten to lock it, so I just came in, and she says please will you see me home when you've finished with me... and I don't suppose you want to see me at all... because... because...it was all my fault about Kinza, and oh, Auntie, whatever shall I do?"

The last words came out with a rush of fresh tears and Aunt Rosemary drew the trembling girl into the room, shut the door and sat down beside her.

"You can't do anything, Jenny," she said gently, "but God loves Kinza far more than we do, and he can do everything. Let's kneel down and ask God together to shelter little Kinza and comfort her and keep her safe."

So they knelt side by side, and Aunt Rosemary prayed that Jesus would protect Kinza. Jenny listened and wondered, more miserable than she had ever been before. It was all very well for Aunt Rosemary, she thought to herself. When dreadful things happened to her, she had a place where she could find forgiveness and peace and comfort. But Jenny knew no such refuge. She felt shut out in the dark. She would never forgive herself, and neither would anyone else, if Kinza was really lost.

For the first time in her life her naughtiness had really mattered, and there seemed no escape from the terrible results of it. Nearly every day she was self-willed and lost her temper if she couldn't get what she wanted. But Mummy and Daddy were always nice and understanding about it, and remembered that after all she had been ill for three months. Now she had gone her own way and disobeyed once too often.

"If only Kinza could come back," said Jenny to herself, "I would never be disobedient or naughty again. I'd be good for ever and ever."

Chapter Sixteen

Rescue plans

Rosemary spent most of the next day trying to trace Hamid, but Hamid was apparently determined not to be traced. Why should the English nurse want him urgently just then? Perhaps his father had spoken to her and she was going to hand him over. It was all most suspicious and Hamid decided to keep clear of her.

However, the English nurse was so determined to find him that, on being told that Hamid had gone up into the mountains early, she cancelled her boys' meeting and settled herself just before sunset behind the pillar of the great stone archway through which he was likely to return. Before long a weary little figure skulked in through the shadows and she grabbed hold of him by what remained of his shirt.

For a moment he struggled violently, but she

spoke to him at once, and her words stopped him immediately and he stood still. "Hamid," she was saying pleadingly, "I've lost Kinza. Please can you help me to find her again? Do you know where she might have gone to?"

She kept tight hold of him and he stood rigidly in front of her, gazing up at her uncertainly. At first he was too startled to think, but gradually his mind cleared, and he began to put two and two together. If Kinza had disappeared, her step-father had certainly taken her home, and if the nurse was searching for her, then she did not know about their step-father. But it did not seem safe to tell; it might lead to contact with the police, and no little street boy ever wishes to have anything to do with the police. Or it might lead to meeting his family – or it might all be a trick or a trap. It was far safer to deny everything and have nothing to do with it.

And yet if he refused to speak, Kinza was lost, and all his efforts were wasted. Kinza had been so happy, so healthy, so safe. Now she would be sold to the beggar – why else should his step-father want her? – and he would not be there to protect her.

"I don't know anything about it," he said warily, after a long pause, but the nurse felt quite sure that he knew a great deal about it – though it might be difficult to worm it out of him, and she must proceed very carefully.

"Let's go home and have some supper together," she said soothingly, "and we can talk about it in the house. You must be hungry after being on the mountain all day."

Since he had had little to eat since the evening

before, having not been to work, he was ravenously hungry. There was a gnawing pain inside him, and unless he accepted the English nurse's offer there was very little chance of food that night. It was rather risky to go to her house, because after all it might be a trick. But he was *so* hungry!

Nobody could make him talk, he thought to himself, so he slipped a dirty little hand into the hand of the English nurse, and she clasped it firmly and did not let go until they were safely inside her house with the door locked behind them.

She led Hamid upstairs to the room where he had once seen Kinza asleep, and he sat down cross-legged on the mat sniffing the delicious smell of hot rice and vegetables cooking in the pot on the fire. She brought him a steaming bowlful and a great hunk of bread, and then fetched her own. She did not question him while he ate, for he was completely absorbed in his food, but she watched him thoughtfully. He was so like Kinza in looks – the same dark, bright eyes, heart-shaped face and determined mouth. She waited until the last drop of food had gone, and the bowl wiped clean with a crust of bread, and then she spoke with a certainty that she did not feel.

"Hamid," she said very firmly, "do you know who has stolen away your little sister Kinza? If you know, you must tell me, because I want to get her back again."

The English nurse was very tired, very strained and very afraid that her guess was wrong. Her voice, which had been quite firm, quivered a little as she finished speaking, and that quiver reassured Hamid. This was no trick. It was the honest cry of a loving heart.

"I think my step-father has got her," he replied. "I saw him watching her in the market yesterday. He followed her right across the square, but I thought she was safe with you."

The nurse was surprised by her success, but she did not show it. She went on speaking very quietly. "Where does your step-father live?"

Hamid told her the name of the village.

"Didn't he know she was with me?"

"No."

The nurse made another guess.

"Why did you put her in my passage that night?"

"My mother told me to."

"Why?"

"My step-father did not want Kinza. He was going to sell her to a beggar. Kinza would have been very unhappy, so my mother sent her to you."

"And now?"

"My step-father will sell her to the beggar. He wants the money."

The nurse shuddered. Kinza's prospects were far worse than she had imagined, and she must save her somehow. She went on quietly questioning: "How far is the village?"

"Two days' journey on a horse – but my father probably came by road on a market lorry. That only takes about six hours."

"And you – how did you come?"

"Partly on a lorry, mostly walking."

"And Kinza?"

"On my back."

The nurse marvelled at his courage; surely

Hamid, who had dared so much for Kinza's sake, would help her now!

"And if I went to your village, and offered to pay your father more than the beggar, would he let me buy back Kinza?"

"I don't know; he might. But how would you know the house? There are many parts of the village with hills between."

"You must come with me and show me."

"I can't. My step-father would beat me dreadfully if I went home."

"You need not come home. You can point out the house from a distance."

"But everyone in the village knows me. They will tell my father."

"We will arrive after sunset in Mr and Mrs Swift's car. No one will see you in the dark. Surely you will do this to save Kinza?"

Hamid scratched his head doubtfully, battling with his fears.

"Hamid," she pleaded, "if you refuse I shan't be able to find her. The beggar will have her, and she will suffer and be cold and hungry in the streets of a big city, and all her life she'll live in the dark. If she comes back to me she will grow up happily, and I will teach her about the Lord Jesus, and how he loves her. I've told you about him so often, Hamid. Do you believe in him yet?"

He glanced up at her shyly but his eyes were bright.

"I love the Lord Jesus very much," he replied simply. "He has forgiven me for all I have done wrong, and made my heart happy."

"Then he can also make your heart brave," she

urged. "Let's ask him now, Hamid, to take away your fear and to save Kinza."

He shut his eyes obediently and as the nurse prayed he repeated the words after her. While he was speaking, two thoughts came into his mind. If the Lord Jesus really loved him he would not let his step-father beat him, and so there was nothing to be afraid of. He also thought what fun it would be to drive all the way to his village in the Englishman's big, fast, grey car.

Even while he prayed, the Spirit of God breathed happy, brave thoughts into his troubled heart, so when they had finished praying he was quite ready to agree to the nurse's suggestions, and he finally left the house feeling very excited. As he wandered across the market-place he imagined himself sitting upright at the car window, waving proudly like a king to his friends. He suddenly laughed with delight and skipped in the air. His step-father would do anything for money, and the nurse would certainly offer more than the beggar would give.

As soon as he had left the house, Rosemary set off for the hotel to discuss her plan with Mr and Mrs Swift. They had taken Jenny up into the mountains for a picnic, but she had not wanted to go and had been in a bad mood all day.

She found them sitting in the lounge looking tired and depressed.

"Has anything happened?" they asked eagerly, jumping up as soon as they saw her.

"Yes," said Rosemary, unable to hide her excitement. She dropped into an empty chair, and leaning forward, she poured out the wonderful story.

"Of course, I've gone and fixed it all up with Hamid without consulting you," she ended, "but I felt quite sure you'd be willing, because you've been so concerned about Kinza. We would have to start tomorrow afternoon – it's about six hours' drive – in order to arrive after sunset. Then Hamid says it's a good walk on beyond where the car can go. We would not be back till after midnight, but I didn't think you'd mind that for once."

"Of course not," Mrs Swift assured her, as eager as she was. "John shall take you and Hamid, and I'll stay with Jenny. I don't think she ought to go."

"There'll be no end of trouble if she's left behind," said her father, and the eagerness vanished from their faces and they both sighed.

"Is Jenny in bed?" enquired Rosemary. "Could I tell her all about it, or will she be asleep?"

Mr and Mrs Swift glanced at each other, and there was a moment's silence. Then Mrs Swift spoke.

"Yes, do go and tell her," she said, "and, Rosemary, I wish you could somehow talk her into a better mood. She's so fond of you, and I don't seem to be able to do anything with her tonight. We've had such a miserable day because she didn't want to come for the picnic. She wanted to stay and help you look for Kinza. Of course, I know she's been ill and all that, but really she does behave like a spoilt baby when she can't get her own way."

"So I sent her to bed when we got in," added Mr Swift gloomily. "Her tempers are just getting too much. She's not used to being punished and took it very badly, so I don't know what sort of mood you'll find her in. She'll certainly kick up an awful fuss if she's not allowed to go tomorrow."

"Poor Jenny!" said Aunt Rosemary. "I'll go and see if she's still awake," and she climbed the stairs rather slowly and knocked at the door. There was no answer. She opened the door and went in.

"What do you want?" said a sullen voice from under the bedclothes. "I haven't gone to sleep early like you said, so you needn't think I have."

"It's me, Jenny," said Aunt Rosemary quietly, and went over and sat down on the bed.

Jenny came out at once, rather embarrassed, for she always spoke politely in front of Aunt Rosemary, wanting her to think she was a nice child. However, Mummy and Daddy had probably been talking about her, and she must make Aunt Rosemary see her point of view. Surely she would understand and see how ill-treated she was.

"Oh, Auntie Rosemary," cried Jenny, bursting into tears; "I'm so glad you've come! I've been thinking about Kinza all day long."

"Oh, no, you haven't," replied Aunt Rosemary in a very matter-of-fact voice. "You've been thinking about yourself all day long, and that's why you're so unhappy. Selfish people are always unhappy because they mind so much when they can't have their own way."

"I'm *not* selfish," sobbed Jenny angrily. "You don't understand any more than Mummy and Daddy do. I couldn't stop wondering where Kinza was, and they took me right away where I couldn't find out or hear if there was any news."

"But your hearing the news wouldn't have helped Kinza at all," replied Aunt Rosemary. "It would just have satisfied your own curiosity. And because you couldn't be satisfied you made Mummy and Daddy miserable all day long, and if that's not selfish I don't know what is."

Jenny could think of nothing to say to that, so she just repeated, "You don't understand."

"Oh, Jenny, Jenny, I understand so well," cried Aunt Rosemary, suddenly kneeling down and drawing the angry, hot little girl towards her. "I understand that because you have always had everything you want, and because Mummy and Daddy have always given you such lovely things, and been so good to you, you think nothing matters in the world except your own happiness. Your heart is like a little closed-in circle with yourself in the middle, and every time something happens that hurts or annoys you, you think the world is coming to an end. And as you get older, Jenny, you will find that there are more and more things that will annoy and hurt you, and you are going to grow into a very unhappy, unloving person. You see, you haven't really time or room to love anyone else properly because you're too busy loving only yourself."

Jenny was quite silent. No one had ever talked to her like this before. Her mother and father usually ended by saying, "Never mind, darling; we're sure you didn't mean it. Let's forget all about it."

But perhaps Auntie Rosemary was partly speaking the truth. She often did feel very, very unhappy, simply because it was not always possible for her to have her own way. She thought of a girl at school who had wanted to learn to ride a horse, and who had wanted a new dress for a party, but she couldn't have either because her father couldn't afford it. Yet she had not made a fuss about it and had seemed to really enjoy the party even though she was wearing one of her sister's old dresses. Jenny could not understand it.

"I can't help minding things," said Jenny at last, in a small, hurt voice. "And I do love people. I love Mummy and Daddy and you and Kinza and lots of people."

"Only as long as we please you," replied Aunt Rosemary. "As soon as we stop doing what you want, you are quite happy to make us miserable, as you've made Mummy and Daddy miserable today."

Jenny was silent again. It was no good trying to make Aunt Rosemary like her, because apparently she knew all about her, but it made her feel peaceful in a strange kind of way. Jenny suddenly felt she could stop pretending.

"I *do* want to be good and happy," she whispered, "and I *do* want to make Mummy happy. But I can't. I just seem to mind things so much that I can't help being cross."

"Yes," agreed Aunt Rosemary thoughtfully, "I know. The only way you can change is to ask Jesus into your heart, and he will come into the circle and help to change you. At first you will still want to have your own way, but the more you love him, the less you will love yourself first. You will want what he wants, and gradually you will become happier and happier and feel more satisfied. It sounds difficult, but it's really quite simple."

"Oh, I see," said Jenny rather sleepily. She had stopped crying and was lying very still. Aunt

Rosemary waited a moment and then said, "I really came to tell you some news of Kinza. We've discovered where she's gone, and tomorrow your father and Hamid and I are going to her home, and we are going to try to persuade her step-father to let us have her back."

"Oh, where? When? How?" cried Jenny, springing up in bed. "Tell me all about it, quickly! Can I come, too?"

"No," said Aunt Rosemary, "you can't. Mummy says we will get back too late, and probably the fewer of us that go the better. You've got a chance to make up for today by obeying without being cross and sulky. Now I'll tell you how I found out, and all about it," and as she told her, Jenny lay and listened quietly.

It was all going to come right after all, perhaps, and she did not deserve it. Last night she had made a sort of promise – "If Kinza comes back I'm going to be good for ever and ever."

"Auntie," she whispered, her face half-buried in the pillow, "tell Mummy to come. I want to tell her I'm sorry, and that I'll be good tomorrow."

Chapter Seventeen

An exciting night

The next day dawned bright and clear, and the rescue party set off early in the afternoon. Jenny, desperately disappointed that she wasn't going too, but determined to make the best of it, stood and waved them off. Hamid, all his fears forgotten in the thrill of being inside the beautiful car, sat in the back seat like a prince and nodded proudly to the crowd of open-mouthed, admiring urchins running behind. Far down the road they followed, shouting and hooting, rags fluttering. Hamid stuck his head far out of the window and yelled with triumph, and Rosemary pulled him in again by the seat of his trousers.

It was a beautiful drive. Hamid remembered the hot, dusty evening when he had toiled up the same hill with Kinza on his back. He had been too tired then to look about him and admire the view, but now he wanted to see everything, and he leapt from side to side of the car like a monkey in a cage.

Later he slept, curled up on the back seat, and when he woke he found the car had stopped in an area surrounded by mountains, and the Englishman and the nurse were drinking tea and eating sandwiches. Hamid was given a sugar bun, and he thought he was in heaven.

Only one thought spoiled his pleasure. As the sun sank towards the western mountains, the grey car was travelling toward his village and his step-father. The big Englishman and the nurse had promised that he would be kept safe, so he was not really very afraid. He laid his head on his arms on the window ledge, thinking. He was coming near to his mother, too, and his heart cried out for her. It would be hard to be so close and yet be unable to see her or speak to her. Two big tears brimmed up in his eyes and trickled over on to the shiny leather car seats.

After a while the car turned off the main road on to a stony mountain road, travelling more slowly between scrubby hills where the villages of the mountain people nestled. Children were bringing their goats home, and several times the car had to stop while a small figure and its flock crossed the road.

Then the sun set behind the hills, and Hamid could see the shape of his own home mountain in the distance with two bright stars twinkling above it. His heart began to beat very fast and his mouth felt rather dry.

It was quite dark when they reached the familiar

market-place. They drove beyond the few shops to where the rough road dwindled into a track, and there Mr Swift stopped the car.

Hamid tumbled out and ran behind an olive tree while the nurse spoke to a boy standing in the doorway of a house, and asked him to mind the car. He knew this boy, and did not wish to be recognised by anyone, so he waited until the boy's back was turned, and then came skulking out from his hiding place and without a word set off quickly along the familiar path, with Mr Swift and the nurse hurrying along behind him. This was the very track up which he had toiled on hot summer evenings carrying Kinza home from market; here was the fountain where he and Rahma had filled buckets at sunrise; to his left was the burying ground, with the three little graves where the marigolds grew, and there in front of him, at the top of the hill, gleamed the lights in the cottages on the outskirts of the village. Just another fifty yards' climb and he could see his own lamp-lit doorway and the rosy glow of the charcoal fire. He stopped short and beckoned his followers to his side.

"There," he breathed, pointing towards it. "It is the third house beyond the fig tree. You just push the gate open – there is no latch. Don't be afraid of the dog – he's chained – and remember you have promised not to tell my step-father."

"Yes, Hamid," said the nurse quietly, "I've promised, and if he comes with us to the car you must just hide until he goes away. We will not leave without you. Otherwise we'll meet you here."

They went cautiously on up the rocky path and

Hamid went off to hide himself safely behind the bushes at the bottom of the burying ground. Crouching there, hugging his knees, he remembered his first escape, when he had crept down the hill at midnight and felt so afraid of evil spirits in the dark. Suddenly he realized he was not afraid any more, and then remembered why. Death was no longer a place of shadows and lost spirits – it was simply a door into the light and sunshine of God's home, and the nurse had said that little children who had no knowledge of good and evil were welcome there, so probably his little brothers and sister were safe and happy after all. Hamid suddenly wished he could go there, too, instead of crouching like an outcast within sight of his own home. He longed for the warm fireside, for the nuzzling goats, for Rahma and, above all, for his mother. His heart strained towards her. Surely she would hear and come?

Mr Swift and Rosemary made their way by torchlight, in single file, along the mud track that led to Hamid's home.

Nobody saw them passing, and when they reached the gate, it was as he had said. It opened with a gentle push, and they stepped out of the shadows and stood hesitating in the light that streamed through the open doorway.

There was the rattle of a chain and the big black dog leaped up and strained on its lead. The bearded man sitting just inside glanced out, saw them, and rose instantly and crossed the hut. There seemed to be a sort of scuffle inside, a quick murmur of low voices, and then the master of the house appeared, smiling and bowing and full of polite greetings. He begged his guests to enter and tell their business inside, and to share their meal, even though the food was poor. Stooping, they passed through the low doorway and stood in the tiny dim room, looking round.

There was a young woman with a sad, patient face squatting by the fire and a shy little dark-eyed girl nestling against her. In a shadowed corner, leaning against a bundled-up blanket, sat an older woman. She did not come forward to greet them; she remained in her corner, silent and watchful, and the master spread a sheepskin on the floor and asked his guests to sit down with their backs to her.

There was no sign of Kinza at all, and the nurse's heart sank – perhaps they had all come on a wild-goose chase.

Expressing polite surprise at the late hour of their visit, the black-bearded man told the young woman to serve them with sweet mint tea, and as they sipped he asked why they had come.

"I have come to find out about your little blind girl, Kinza," replied the nurse, speaking very firmly. "She was left in my charge by her brother about seven months ago. I have grown very fond of the child, and would very much like to have her back. She is your child, and it must be as you wish, but I am willing to pay a price for her – and of course her mother can come and see her from time to time."

There was an instant's silence while Si Mohamed, completely taken by surprise by the assurance in her voice, hesitated. She had mentioned paying a price, and he would do almost anything for money; she would pay more than the beggar. On the other hand, he might get into trouble for having taken her, and there was the question of her fine clothes. Kinza had arrived home after dark, wrapped in a potato sack, and had been kept out of sight ever since. He had sold her clothes to some Spaniards that very morning. It was too much to risk. He pretended to look surprised and spread out his hands, palm upwards.

"But I don't know where she is," he assured her in an injured voice. "True, her brother stole her away about seven months ago, but since then I have neither seen her nor received news of her. If the boy has told you that this is her home, he is speaking the truth, but the child is not here. If I hear news of her, I will gladly bring her to you."

There was a long pause. Rosemary's eyes met the eyes of the young woman sitting at the other side of the fire. They were fixed on her very steadily and – was it imagination, or did she really give a very faint nod in the direction of the old woman?

Rosemary turned on her sheepskin and looked all round the room. There was only one possible place for Kinza to be hidden, and that was under the blanket behind the old woman. No longer caring anything about manners, she got up suddenly and stepped across the room, and called out Kinza's name at the top of her voice three times over.

The man stood on his feet, pale with fright; the old woman clutched at the blanket, but she was too late. At the sound of the well-known, well-loved voice, Kinza sprang up with a loud answering cry and frantically struggled out from under the blanket. Rosemary almost lifted the old woman out of the way, and the next moment Kinza was in her arms, clinging to her as though she would never let go.

Kinza's joy was indescribable; all the terror was over and she was safe again in the arms of her protector. The last two-and-a-half days had been a nightmare of jolting and cold, as she had lain all night wrapped in a sack on the boards of a lorry-trailer, of smacks when she cried, of hunger and fear and bewilderment, and of rough hands that had snatched her from her mother's arms. But that was all over now. Her strained body relaxed and she lay at peace. Rosemary turned to face the step-father.

He had risen threateningly, his face pale with anger and fear, and Mr Swift had risen too and stood ready to act if necessary. He was a big man, and Si Mohamed realised in a moment that his only hope now was to give in graciously and strike a good bargain.

"There," he said rather nervously, "you have found her, and now she will be your daughter. You are very welcome to her, and with you I know she will be safe and happy. Now tell me what are you willing to pay for her?"

Rosemary mentioned a sum much higher than Hamid had told her the beggar had offered. Si Mohamed, terrified that her clothes were going to be mentioned and only anxious to get rid of his unwelcome guests, accepted the offer at once.

He came forward to receive the money, with expressions of delight that Kinza should be so honoured, and Kinza screamed when she heard the dreaded voice approaching.

Rosemary handed over the money and bent over the frightened child. "It's all right, Kinza," she whispered. "Don't be afraid. He can't touch you. You're my little girl now."

Reassured and trustful, Kinza stuck two fingers in her mouth and lay still, content and unafraid in the arms of her friend. She was soon fast asleep. She did not know that a long journey and been taken for her sake and that a high price had been paid to buy her back again, but the voice that had never yet told her a lie had said, "Don't be afraid; you're my little girl now."

There was nothing left to do but get away as quickly as possible before any further trouble arose. Rosemary said a brief goodbye to the old woman and the step-father and turned to speak to the mother, but her seat by the charcoal pot was empty. Only the little girl sat watching, solemn and big-eyed. The mother had slipped out unnoticed while the payment was being arranged, and, caring nothing for her husband's anger, she was hurrying down the steep path that led from the village, calling softly and breathlessly to her son.

She guessed he must be near, for how else could they have found their way to the house? But even so she was startled when a little figure ran out from the shadows of the olive trees on the outskirts of the burying ground, and kissed her hand. She pulled him fearfully back into the dark safety of the trees and looked into his upturned face. "Little son, little son," she whispered, for she knew their time was short, "how are you? Are you all right?"

"I'm fine," he whispered back. "I work in the town and all is well. But Kinza – have they got her?"

His mother nodded. "The English woman paid a price for her and will take her as her daughter. I have no more fear for Kinza. All will be well for her and she will never suffer or be beaten or beg. But you, little son... come back to me. I miss you so."

He shook his head slowly. "I daren't," he breathed. "Si Mohamed would kill me with beating. I have work and can live, and the English nurse feeds us at night. Besides, she has a book about Jesus, the man she told you about who took children in his arms, and in that book is written the way of God which leads to heaven. What she tells us from her book makes my heart happy and I must know more."

He was speaking very earnestly and she drew him close against her. He had grown taller, but he was so thin, and to her he still seemed such a little boy; yet all on his own he had found happiness. She could see his face brighten in the moonlight as he spoke. If only she could follow him. She had no happiness.

"Then you must come and tell me, little son," she urged. "I want to be happy too. Your step-father won't beat you. He has to pay a boy to look after his goats, and he often grumbles because you are not here to work for him. He would be glad to see you back."

He rested his head against her shoulder and sat very still, thinking hard. He was tired of travelling and wandering and fending for himself, tired of trying to be a man before his time. All he wanted was to be a little boy again, and lean unashamed against his mother in the dark for a while and then to go home.

But if he did that, he would never learn to read from the nurse's book and perhaps he would forget the way to heaven. Besides, he was still very afraid of his step-father. Slowly, and after a long silence, he made up his mind.

"I will go back now," he whispered, "and I'll learn to read from the book that tells the way to heaven. Then when the harvest is ripe I'll come and tell you all about it. Only ask Si Mohamed not to beat me."

Steps sounded on the path and the light of a torch was flashed on to them. They rose quickly and came out into the open moonlight. The mother stooped and kissed her sleeping baby quickly, whispered a blessing on the nurse and gave her hand to her son. Then without another word she turned up the hill and went back to the punishment that awaited her, content and unafraid. Kinza was safe for ever, and she had seen her little boy. All was well with him and he had promised to come home. Nothing else mattered.

The little party hurried towards the valley. Mr Swift carried Kinza and Rosemary held the torch; Hamid bounded ahead, knowing every inch of the way. They had almost reached the car when they heard quick steps behind them and angry shouting. It was Si Mohamed, coming after his runaway boy. His wife's disappearance had roused his suspicions. The quiet joy in her face on her return had confirmed them.

"My step-father!" gasped Hamid and he made for the car like a hunted rabbit. Finding the door locked, he stood jumping up and down, squeaking with fear. The nurse was only a few seconds behind him, and the big Englishman tossed Kinza into her arms as though she was a bundle of washing, jammed the key in the lock, dived into the front, started the car and opened the back doors. The nurse, Kinza and Hamid all seemed to fall in at once as the car moved off with a triumphant roar. It shot past the empty market-place, bumping horribly, leaving Si Mohamed standing alone under the eucalyptus trees, very angry and out of breath, while his step-son flung himself back against the shiny cushions and started to laugh.

Five minutes later they had all settled themselves comfortably and got over their fright. Kinza slept deeply and peacefully, worn out by the terror and uncertainty of the past three days. Hamid rested his brown arms on the window, and his gaze wandered to the twin peaks above his home. He knew that he would come back, alone and on foot, one summer evening when the fields were ripe for harvest. And he would not feel afraid, for Jesus had said: "No follower of mine shall wander in the dark; he shall have the light of life."*

* John 8:12 New English Bible.

Chapter Eighteen

New beginnings

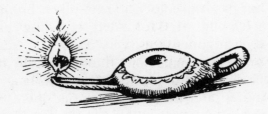

While Mr Swift, Rosemary and Hamid had rescued Kinza, Jenny had spent a long, long day at the hotel. It was a day in which she had plenty of time to think.

She wished she knew more about the Lord Jesus, and had a Bible so she could read about him. She thought about the picture in the clinic, and it reassured her that he loved children and wanted to come into her heart and change her. Instead of being cross, spoilt and vain, she could be strong and happy and loving. "Like putting a candle inside an empty lantern, so that the light shines out," Aunt Rosemary had said.

"Lord Jesus, please come into my life," Jenny prayed now.

That night she had so much to think about that she was sure she would never go to sleep, and yet her eyes closed almost immediately, and the next thing she knew was that her mother was shaking her gently. Auntie Rosemary was sitting at the foot of the bed laughing and holding a bundle wrapped up in the car-rug in her arms.

"It's Kinza!" cried Jenny, flinging herself on the bundle and hugging and kissing her. It was only two o'clock in the morning, so they had to talk in whispers because of the other guests, but Jenny wanted to know all about the rescue.

Everyone was hungry, so they made some tea. Mrs Swift spread butter and honey on some bread, and passed round biscuits. Never had there been a happier midnight feast, and Jenny knew that she would remember that hour all her life. Kinza had been brought back, and all Jenny's naughtiness had been forgiven and forgotten. She was going to start again, a new child in a new happy life. Sitting there in bed with all the people she loved best grouped around her, and her mouth full of bread and honey, she felt so happy she thought she would burst. Her mother said rather weakly four times that they really must all go to bed, but no one took the slightest notice; they just went on eating and whispering. When Mr Swift told them how they had escaped from Si Mohamed, he fell backwards in his excitement. Everyone tried so hard not to laugh out loud, then Kinza woke and sat up, blinking at them solemnly like a baby owl. She didn't seem to like all this midnight merriment, for after a few moments she cuddled back in the rug and went to sleep again. Then Mrs Swift said for the fifth time that they really must go to bed and Mr Swift said, "All right, but let me just have one more piece of bread because falling off the bed made me hungry again," and then Aunt Rosemary wanted another piece, and so did Jenny, and her mother thought she might as well have one, too.

Then Mrs Swift said for the sixth time that they really must go to bed, and this time they *did* listen to her. They all kissed Jenny goodnight and tucked her up in turn, and then went off down the passage laughing at Mr Swift, who was trying to walk quietly in his enormous squeaky shoes, like an elephant trying to walk on tiptoe. Jenny was left alone with her happiness. God had heard their prayers, and Kinza had come back.

Everyone slept on next morning till the sun was high – except Hamid and Aunt Rosemary. They got up at the usual time, Hamid because he had slept well all night on the back seat of Mr Swift's car, and Rosemary because she had a busy day ahead of her. It was still quite early when she was disturbed by a loud knocking, and she got up with a little sigh. When she opened the door, she found Hamid, his hands and face pink and shining from washing in the fountain.

His rags were dreadfully torn and dirty, and he had nasty sores on his legs, but the child was as eager and full of life as the spring morning. He kissed the nurse's hand, chuckled, and hopped uninvited over the threshold. He seemed to have come for a particular reason, but didn't know what to say. "How's Kinza?" he enquired.

"She's all right," said the nurse. "Do you want to come and see her?"

For an answer he skipped upstairs ahead of her to where Kinza lay in her old corner on the mat, her dark head pillowed on her arm, fast asleep. Hamid nodded, well pleased, and then looked around hopefully to see if there was any chance of something to eat. He had timed his visit perfectly, for the English nurse was just in the middle of her breakfast. Hamid sat cross-legged on the floor with bright, hopeful eyes. He had not eaten honey sandwiches in the night, and he was very hungry.

The nurse gave him a bowl of sweet coffee and a big hunk of bread. He sipped it noisily, chuckling with pleasure between mouthfuls. When he had finished and cleaned out the bowl with his finger for fear of wasting any sugar, he came a little closer and said confidently, "Teach me to read."

The nurse looked at him doubtfully. "But so many people want to learn to read and they only keep it up for about a fortnight. Then my time is all wasted."

Hamid shook his head very firmly. "I would go on every day, until harvest time," he said, "because then I am going home. My step-father will be glad to see me at harvest because he's so busy. Could I learn to read before harvest?"

"I should think so," replied the nurse, "if you really come every day." She thought of her busy days and wondered when she would fit him in, but the child seemed so keen and determined.

"Why do you want to learn to read, Hamid?" she asked.

He lifted a serious brown face to hers and told her his simple little story.

"I want to go home," he said. "But if I go home and can't read, who will go on teaching me the way to heaven?"

"Then you believe it really is the way to heaven?"

"Yes; I had a dream. I saw the Lord Jesus with his arms stretched out. I think he was on a cross. And behind the cross was a door, wide open, and he told me it was the way to God. And he told me I was to come to you because it was all written down in your book."

"Very well," said the nurse quietly. "You can come every day just about this time. We'll start at once."

She fetched her book of Arabic letters and found him a very quick pupil. By the end of half an hour he had learned quite a number of letters and was really pleased with himself.

"Aa -d -dd -rr -z," he chanted proudly. "Now I can read!"

He skipped off with his head held high, and the nurse went back with a happy heart to clear the breakfast things.

Chapter Nineteen

Aunt Rosemary explains

It was very nearly the end of the holiday now, and on the last Saturday they all started off early in the morning and went for a picnic far up in the mountains with a fat picnic basket.

They drove up and up past thatched villages until the road plunged down into the cool shadow of pine woods, where English primroses grew round the roots of the giant trees.

Jenny and Aunt Rosemary started picking bunches of the pale yellow flowers. Jenny wanted to tell her aunt her new secret. She must try to tell her today because there might not be another chance, but she did not know how to begin to say it. She prayed for the right opportunity to talk to her aunt. She was sure something very important had happened to her, and wanted Aunt Rosemary to tell her what to expect next. The day passed, and she just didn't seem to find the right moment to ask her.

They drove home in the evening, Jenny's head leaning against her father's shoulder. She was disappointed because she had not managed to speak to her aunt, and doubts were beginning to creep in. They were driving through a low water-meadow, with white lilies growing in clumps by the river. Jenny suddenly remembered that the next day would be Easter Sunday, and she sat up quickly.

Jenny liked Easter Sunday. There were always white flowers on the breakfast table, and big coloured Easter eggs round her plate. After breakfast they would go to church, which was decorated with white lilies and narcissi and bright daffodils, and the choir boys in white robes sang "Jesus Christ is risen today... Alleluia!"

Here they would not go to church because there was no church to go to, but Jenny decided she could visit Aunt Rosemary early with some white flowers, and perhaps then she could tell her her secret. She laid her hand on her father's arm.

"Stop, Daddy," she said.

Mr Swift stopped. "What's up?" he enquired.

"I want to get something," Jenny explained. She jumped out of the car and ran backwards a little so that they could not see what she was doing. She raced across the field, gathered an armful of lilies from the water's edge, wrapped them in her sweater and raced back to the car.

"What have you got there, Jenny?" asked her father.

"A secret," replied Jenny. "We can go on now!"

Mrs Swift, who had been watching her nimble little daughter through the back window, smiled and said nothing. It was not till Jenny was tucked in bed and the flowers were up to their necks in the water-jug that she understood what it was all about.

"Mummy," said Jenny, "it's Easter Sunday tomorrow, and on Easter Sunday there are always white flowers. Can I get up very early and take my lilies to Aunt Rosemary as an Easter surprise?"

"Of course," answered her mother, "What a lovely idea. She has been so kind to you, Jenny. You can go when you wake up. I expect you'll stay and have breakfast with her. I'll put your clean clothes out now."

She laid out Jenny's best dress and clean socks, kissed her goodnight and left her, and Jenny went to sleep at once, looking forward to the morning. Perhaps it was all going to come right after all.

She woke very early, just at the time when in England the church bells would start ringing to remind people that Jesus Christ had risen. She jumped out of bed, washed and dressed herself extra carefully because it was Easter Day, and set off.

She knocked at the door and Auntie Rosemary, who was up having her breakfast, appeared at the window, surprised at such an early caller. Seeing who it was she ran down to open the door, and Jenny bounded joyfully in and held up her bouquet.

"White flowers for Easter!" she announced triumphantly. "I picked them yesterday without you seeing me."

They went upstairs to where breakfast was laid on a white cloth, with a bowl of primroses in the middle of the table. They arranged Jenny's flowers in a vase behind the primroses and sat down to enjoy themselves.

"It looks like a church at Easter-time, doesn't it?" remarked Jenny. "On Easter Sunday at home, Mummy, Daddy and I always go to church. It's a pity there isn't a church here, isn't it, so we could all go together?"

"Yes," answered her aunt, "I really miss going to church, and yet you know, Jenny, it doesn't really matter in one way. The main reason for going to church is to meet God, and we can meet God any-where. I meet him here every day in my room; just now when you came I was reading the Easter story in my Bible."

"Will you read it to me if you've finished eat-ing?" asked Jenny eagerly, settling herself very comfortably to listen while Aunt Rosemary read to her.

"Jesus met Mary in the garden," said Aunt Rosemary; "and he met some of the disciples in a little room, and he met two others on the road, and he met Peter on the beach. So you see it isn't really necessary to go to a building."

"No," said Jenny simply, lifting a bright face; "that's what I wanted to tell you. The other day... the day you went to fetch Kinza... I thought he met me, up on the hillside. I asked Jesus to come and live inside me like the light in the lantern, and stop me being selfish and cross. And I felt so happy and I thought he had come. But yesterday I began to wonder if it was all really true. Do you think he really came, Auntie, because I don't really *feel* very different."

Aunt Rosemary was silent for a moment. Then she said quietly, "Jenny, how did Mary feel quite sure that Jesus had really come to her?"

"When he said her name," answered Jenny. "It was easy for her. She heard him and saw him."

"Yes, I know," said Aunt Rosemary, "but it's really quite easy for us too if only we believe that God speaks the truth. I'm going to read you something, Jenny, and then I'm going to tell you a story."

"Good," said Jenny, who loved stories, and she wriggled close to look over Auntie Rosemary's Bible. They read Isaiah chapter 43 verse 1:

"The Lord says: 'Don't be afraid, for I have redeemed you, I have called you by name; you are mine.'"

"That verse reminds me of Kinza the night we went to look for her," said Aunt Rosemary, glancing at the hump in the corner where Kinza was sleeping. "She was living with me quite happily, but she was stolen, and taken away from me. I love Kinza very much and I knew she'd be unhappy, so I went after her, and I found her hungry and frightened and wanting me. She didn't know I was there, but I knew she was there, so what did I do?"

"Shouted her name!" said Jenny, with sparkling eyes. She knew this story well, and would never tire of hearing it again.

Aunt Rosemary laughed. "Yes, that's right," she said. "I called her by her name. I said 'Kinza' – and what did Kinza do?"

"Bustled out from under her rug in no time!" cried Jenny.

"Yes, she bustled out in no time," repeated Aunt Rosemary. "She was unhappy and frightened and she knew if she came she would be safe and happy, so she didn't stop to ask how or why or if it really was me. She knew it was me by the way I called her name, and she came straight into my arms and felt perfectly safe; she knew she could trust me. And that's exactly what happened to you on the hill-side, Jenny. You didn't know much about Jesus; you were just miserable and tired of yourself. But Jesus knew all about you and he wanted to make you good and happy. So he called you by your name, and you knew it was him and you came at once and felt perfectly safe."

"Only for two days," answered Jenny.

"Yes, exactly," agreed Aunt Rosemary; "and that's just what happened to Kinza. She hadn't been in my arms two minutes before her step-father began talking, and Kinza began to tremble and cry. I was holding her just as close, and loved her just as much, but as soon as she heard the voice of the man who had stolen her and beaten her she began to feel afraid and wonder if it was all right after all. Sometimes we might worry and feel afraid, and wonder if it's all true. But our feelings don't really matter very much, because Jesus doesn't change. He holds us just as close and loves us just as much whether we worry about it or not."

"Oh, I see," said Jenny thoughtfully.

"Now listen to what happened next. I went up to Si Mohamed and I took some money out of my pocket and paid him, and if Kinza had been old enough to understand I'd have said this: 'Don't be afraid, Kinza, I've redeemed you – that means bought you back again. No one can take you away from me now. You're my little girl for ever. But I did just whisper, 'Don't be afraid, Kinza; you're my little girl now.' And Kinza did a very sensible thing. She believed me and she stopped being afraid. Although that cruel man was still standing in front of her talking, she just clung to me as close as she could and fell quietly asleep in my arms and slept all the way home. And the only way to stop feeling afraid is simply to believe what Jesus says. He rose again on Easter Sunday so that he could live in the hearts of everybody who hears his call and comes to him."

Jenny sat quite silent, thinking over what her aunt had said. She felt perfectly happy because now she understood what had really happened. Jesus had loved her and died for her and paid for her and called her and made her his own. All she had to do was simply to come and believe him.

They talked for quite a while after that, and then Kinza woke up and wanted her breakfast, and Jenny went skipping off through the sunshine to find her father and mother. But Rosemary sat very still watching her curly-headed baby who sat with her face buried in her bowl of milk.

She had felt quite sure for the past few days that it was not safe for Kinza to stay with her any longer. As soon as the step-father wanted more money he could easily come and claim the child. For the next few years she must be taken somewhere out of his reach, and the obvious place was

Jenny's Blind School.

And yet what Aunt Rosemary wanted more than anything else for Kinza was that she be brought up by someone who would teach her to love Jesus while she was still tiny. Now she knew the answer quite clearly. She would ask Jenny to teach Kinza, and pray that the Holy Spirit of God would teach Jenny what to say.

Chapter Twenty

Partings and plans

When Jenny was told that Kinza was going home with them, she nearly went wild with joy and excitement, and danced about like a crazy little lamb. The thought of having Kinza to look after on the journey didn't make it so hard to say goodbye to Aunt Rosemary. It was not going to be a very long goodbye, anyway, as Aunt Rosemary was due home on holiday in the summer, and had promised to come and stay with them all.

The evening before they left, Jenny took her aunt and Kinza for a last walk up the mountain, and they sat there together for a little while watching the sunset.

"Are you sad that Kinza's going away, Auntie?" asked Jenny suddenly.

"Well, of course I will miss her dreadfully, but I

feel quite happy about her. You see, what I want most of all for Kinza is that she learns to know and love the Lord Jesus while she's still tiny, and now that you know him you'll be able to teach her. Of course, I expect she'll learn something at Blind School, but such a small child needs someone special all to herself to teach her."

Jenny looked serious. "I don't know that much myself," she replied doubtfully, "who'll teach me, Auntie Rosemary? At school they don't talk like you do."

"Yes, it does seem difficult," said Aunt Rosemary. "But it's quite all right, because you've got your Bible, and you've got the Holy Spirit of Jesus in your heart to show you what it means and help you understand it."

"There are such long words in it," said Jenny, still doubtful.

"I'm sure you'll find Mummy and Daddy willing to explain hard words if you ask them," answered Aunt Rosemary. "They are interested in everything that interests you. Have you told them what happened to you and why you want to read the Bible?"

"No," said Jenny, frowning, "I wanted to, but somehow I couldn't explain."

"Well, it would be a very good thing to tell them in words," said Aunt Rosemary, "but a far more important way is to show them that you are a changed girl – that Jesus is changing your bad-tempered, selfish ways. And as soon as that begins to happen Mummy and Daddy will know all about it without any telling."

"Yes," agreed Jenny. "They'd certainly be pleased if I really became nice and good and never got into rages, and I expect they'd want to know why, too. I should think I'd better show them first, and then they'll believe me when I tell them. Let's go home now, and I'll show them I want to help with the packing."

Next morning at dawn they all gathered at the hotel door to say goodbye. Hamid appeared to say goodbye to his little sister. Mr and Mrs Swift were busy with porters and bills. While she waited, Aunt Rosemary stood watching the three children whom she had come to love more than any other children she knew. They stood in a little group by the luggage – beautiful, rich Jenny, ragged Hamid and blind Kinza. She wondered what lay ahead of them, and felt thankful that the light of Jesus' love would guide and protect them. One day they would all meet again, in heaven.

A few moments later they had said goodbye and the car drove off towards the green valley. Jenny's eyes were full of tears, but Kinza, beating excitedly on the windows, had not yet realised that Rosemary was not also inside. When she did realise, she would no doubt be comforted quickly with a biscuit. They drove round the corner and out of sight, and Rosemary was comforted to find that one of her children, at least, was still close beside her. One great mission of Hamid's young life had been completely successful, but his little sister would never need him again. She would have fine clothes, big cars and biscuits. Now he had to return to the deserted market-place, hunger, homelessness and rags.

"Come and have breakfast," said the nurse at his side.

He brightened up at once and forgot all his troubles. The thought of hot coffee and bread and butter made the world seem much happier. He raced along beside her, rubbing his hands delightedly. He had no work today because the master had gone to town, so there was plenty of time and, apart from this invitation, little chance of anything to eat.

When breakfast was over he had his daily reading lesson. He was getting on very fast and the nurse marvelled at him. She had taught all types of children and it was amazing how quick the street children were to learn. Their wits and memories were sharpened by the struggle they had to keep alive, and they had trained themselves to look and remember. In a week, Hamid had learnt all his letters and knew the repeating exercises by heart; in fact he was rather boastful about it.

"Now I know everything," he remarked, beaming as he struggled through a few three-letter words.

"Oh, no, Hamid; you are only just beginning. You must practise and practise putting the letters into words, and you must come every day if you want to read the Bible by harvest time."

He nodded confidently.

"By harvest time," he repeated. "Then I shall go back and read the Word of God to my mother. Then she will know the way to heaven too, and even if my step-father beats her and won't give her enough food, the Lord Jesus will make her heart happy."

"Will your step-father let you read the Word of God to her?"

"Oh, no. But I shall read it in the granary when my mother is grinding corn and I shall read to my sister Rahma when we look after the goats on the mountain. Si Mohamed will never know."

"But later on, Hamid, he will have to know, if you are going to follow Jesus faithfully. You will have to tell him and he may beat you. But Jesus suffered a great deal for you because he loved you. If you love him, you must be willing to suffer a little, too."

He turned thoughtful, troubled eyes on her.

"I do love him very much," he said, and got up to go, leaving Rosemary happy with his answer.

It wasn't long before Hamid could read, he worked at it so hard; and to Rosemary it seemed no time at all before she was bringing him his farewell meal of bread and lentils.

Hamid wasn't travelling alone; he had some companions. He had much farther to travel than the others, but packed in with the crusts and the water-bottle and the cherries he carried his precious new Bible – the Word of God, that would guide and protect him. He had Jesus' promise, "I am the light of the world; he that follows me shall not walk in darkness, but shall have the light of life."

Rosemary watched them as they scampered away, and at the end of the street they all turned and waved, five bright little figures black against the sky. Then they turned the corner, and disappeared into the glorious light of the sunset.

To the children who have read this book...

Patricia St John was a very dear friend of mine. I know that the stories she wrote were based on real people and real events, so most of the things that happened in Star of Light are true. Patricia collected lots of incidents from the lives of people she knew and worked with, and wove them into this story.

She was a missionary nurse who worked in North Africa for many years, living in a little house in a mountain village, like Aunt Rosemary in the story. She had 'open house' for street children – mainly boys – and tried to help many people who came to her door for medical assistance, some having travelled long, weary miles. She also trekked many miles through mountain territory herself to visit and care for needy people in remote villages, like Hamid's.

Although in some ways this might seem a sad story, Patricia wrote it with the aim of giving a true picture of what life can be like for many children who live in poor countries, who have never heard about Jesus' love. Amongst the sadness there is hope and joy, as many people, like Hamid, have responded to the message of the gospel by asking Jesus into their hearts, and their lives have been changed for the better.

Patricia hoped that by being informed about the lives of others who are not so fortunate, her readers might be encouraged to pray for them and to become involved in practical ways to show Jesus' love and compassion. She became President of Global Care, a Coventry-based Christian charity which helps needy children in many parts of the world. If you would like to find out more about their work, their address is: Global Care, 2 Dugdale Road, FREEPOST CV2657, Coventry, CV6 1BR.

Patricia's work as a nurse was with an organisation now known as Arab World Ministries. They are still working for the good of children and adults and sharing with them the good news of the love of Jesus. If you would like to know more about them, their address is: Arab World Ministries, PO Box 51, Loughborough, Leicestershire LE11 0ZQ.

Mary Mills

*Other books by Patricia St John
for you to enjoy*

Treasures of the Snow

Annette knew that she
could never forgive Lucien
for what he did to Dani.
And she was going to make
sure tha no one else did
either. But then some
surprising things began to
happen to both of them...

ISBN 1 85999 266 8
£3.99

*You can buy this book at your local Christian
bookshop or online at
www.scriptureunion.org.uk/publishing*

The Tanglewoods' Secret

Ruth was only good at
getting into trouble!
Skipping her housework
jobs to play with her
brother Philip, planning
wild schemes to raise
money for the camera they
both wanted, or simply
being rude to Aunt
Margaret. There seemed to be no end to
her mischief until the day she actually ran
away.

ISBN 1 85999 267 6
£3.99